HOSTEL TO ANOTHER
WORLD

HOSTEL TO ANOTHER WORLD

THE WORLD BENEATH

A. L. SELF

Topsider Books

Contents

One
The Birth of Worlds   1

Two
The Little Creature   6

Three
A Hooman!   10

Four
The Magician's Teapot   16

Five
The Skeleton Banquet   23

Six
The Angel of Death   30

Seven
A Topsider's Plot   37

Eight
When Silver Threads Meet   48

Nine
A Trial by Fire   54

Ten
A Holy Intervention   63

Eleven
Goodbye Old Friends   72

Twelve
A Skeleton Army   76

Thirteen
Yesterday's Enemy, Today's Friend   80

Fourteen
A Sea of Fire   87

Fifteen
The Beginning of the End   93

One

The Birth of Worlds

In the beginning, Kurbaga created the World Above and the World Beneath. Now the World Above was formless and empty, darkness was over the high and the deep, so Kurbaga sat to ponder these things at the very centre of the earth. He was somewhat froglike with green, smooth, shiny skin covering his many limbs. Kurbaga had modelled these limbs to be especially long.

"All the better to climb with," he smiled at himself chuckling.

Judging by the ill formed walls of the half finished cavern before him, this was indeed a wise choice. Kurbaga thought hard, looking from the stalactites to the stalagmites with several sets of piercing yellow eyes, for it was always best to have spares of everything. The most exciting part of Kurbaga's new appearance of course was his golden aura, or little bubble. "Why use limbs when one can float around in a little golden orb? Far more befitting of the Master of Creation."

Ideas and troubles skipped and taunted him as he tried his best to think of only one silly thing at a time. "Kurbaga makes me sound a tad too old," he mused at last, stroking his small silver beard before realising his mistake and quickly disposing of it. "Right, enough of that," he huffed standing up in his bubble. With a great big grin and limbs stretched wide he sang, "Let there be magic!"

Magic popped and whizzed through the caverns of the earth, utterly delighted at the freedom, giving birth to all manners of unusual and wonderful things. Kurbaga saw that the magic was precious, and separated the magic from the grey. "The magic will be called the World Beneath, and the grey, the World Above - Topside for short."

He chuckled at his own genius and sighed. Floating over the power of magic and the simpleness of grey, Kurbaga felt a sense of foreboding. "Well fiddlesticks."

He reached out his webbed hand in haste and commanded with heavy heart, "Let there be locked doors between the worlds, to separate world from world."

Great gates of doors took form between the worlds, and Kurbaga locked them tight, separating the magic below from the grey above. He watched the squirming locks of separation with knowing eyes as the gates groaned with the birth of secrets.

The Master of Creation paused here, realising he had produced twice the work for himself. "Oh bother! What a fool am I!"

At this unfortunate realisation, he took a bone from his chest and breathed life and authority, giving it being. "I will call you Iskelet Kral," smiled Kurbaga, "my Skeleton King".

The bones escaped together, budding from the first, growing upwards to form a body. It only had two legs and two arms - a reserved choice. Kurbaga spoke to his servant, "Kral, I am a busy Master. Go create the World Above as you see fit. Set the land to produce vegetation of various kinds without the need of care or magic."

"It will be so Master," replied Kral leaving in haste.

Kurbaga then happily proceeded to do very little, dropping magic here and there, daydreaming, floating, and falling in love with his world. The World Beneath obediently formed below his feet as he sang nonsense songs, with magical creatures sprouting just about everywhere.

Meanwhile, Kral was working diligently to turn the grey into all manners of colour, careful not to leave any magic behind, just as he had been instructed.

Kral spoke to the emptiness, "Let there be lights in the vault of the sky to separate the day from the night, and let them serve as signs to make uprisings. Let there be order with days and years, and let them give light on this grey earth of mine."

Kral made three great lights - the greater light to govern the day and the lesser light to govern the night. The third would become known as the Twilight, when the locks between worlds would weaken in the face of the secret third light, hidden within the mists. "What is the birth of creation without a little secret?"

He waved his boney fingers like batons with careful magic, creating uncountable stars for future creations. They twinkled like eyes, looking over him as he worked to make Master proud. The Skeleton King sighed, "This grey world that Master has given me is unexciting. The governing lights I created are full yet shrouded and dull, not governing at all. I can do better," he huffed. He reached out to his creation, "Let grey become blue."

The command resonated across the World Above like a gong, springing piercing blue waters and adoring blue skies. "Let the water team with living creatures, and let fish fly across the golden skies knowing no limits."

Kral watched as a shoal of giant guppies soared high trying to catch the golden droplets that had started to fall from the Twilight. He frowned and waved a boney hand over the cracks in the waters that had already started creeping in, sealing them temporarily with a hint of cheeky magic. Kral sent even thicker mists to hide the golden rains of the Twilight World, leaving the blues of Topside to settle for the greater and lesser lights. "Having a job is hard," he exclaimed suddenly as he pondered an eternity of work babysitting such a delicate world.

Hovering over the endless waters, he was struck by a fantastic idea. "What if there were superior beings who could govern the earth for me?"

The Skeleton King did a little twirl. Falling downwards, he began soaring like the fish, hovering over the waters, brushing them with his toes happily. "I will make them in my likeness and they will learn to swim and...land!"

Kral had his next mission at hand. With a quick wave of his bony fingers, the land took shape with an unfair allocation of resources and beauty. "May my future governors learn to rely upon one another, sharing in all that I have given them."

The Skeleton King hovered and tentatively stood upon the edge of his land. "It works!"

With a sigh of relief, Kral paced to work up the courage and magic needed for the birth of his governors. Looking down at the sparkling waters biting his toes, he took notice of his own reflection. The Skeleton King suddenly looked a little troubled. "I do not wish my governing beings to die in fear upon glimpsing my disposition," he reasoned thoughtfully, looking to the creatures who had gathered beside him expectantly.

He set upon his own image. Kral quickly covered himself in skin and fine linen cloths of purple, befitting of a king. Admiring his reflection in the waters, it became quickly apparent that his skeleton was poorly hidden and he was in fact, still very scary. He proceeded to add firm flesh, as if inflating a very stubborn balloon. Kral even fashioned himself a striking printed fur coat, inspired by the Master's. "Perfect!" he laughed delightedly looking to the creatures who helpfully hopped and wriggled their approval.

The Skeleton King swished his coat with a warm hand and lifting the other in a fist, he called and weaved his magic, knitting together his trusted creatures named hoomans. The World Above was gifted to the hoomans to govern with full authority and the creatures humbly accepted their honour.

The Skeleton King was ready to return to his Master and show him all that he had done.

At this, the little creature closed the Book of Origin. *Why spoil the story? Besides, a happy ending isn't happy when you're on the wrong side of history.*

"My Skeleton King," it whispered smiling at the image of Iskelet Kral surrounded by his creatures of Origin.

The tattered book was returned to its sleeping place under the mattress and the little creature stood tall, ready for an adventure of his very own.

Two

The Little Creature

Here is where our story really begins dear reader, at the very peak of history, where beginning and end are close to the touch, and time itself had started guessing. In a house among the clouds there lived a kedi.

What is a kedi? Indeed, kedis are peculiar creatures nowadays, quite rare and most certainly hidden away from Topsiders, as they refer to us. The lucky beings are gifted with features resembling those of the Origin creature named the cat and so look rather dashing I daresay. They hold an ancient kind of magic about them, the kind that plays tricks on the mind. It helps them to disappear and even meddle with reality itself if the user is particularly talented. Swift and nimble, the kedi will disappear into the shadows, especially when dangerous beings such as ourselves start stomping around with huge footsteps.

Now the ordinary little kedi lived in a very ordinary little world. In fact, it quite simply was his favourite little world, hidden away, tucked in between all those pesky real worlds. Well, the little creature saw them as rather pesky. Truth be told, he had never actually been to any of the worlds. According to his memory, he had never even ventured out beyond the many walls of his house in the sky. The little thing smiled. Why would he? The World Beneath never got any rest with all its messy magic and Topside had been sending bombs through the gates again according to the morning paper. Topside was full of evil hungry creatures after their magic. *Selfish boring creatures. Who names themselves hooman of all things? If only Kral had stopped at the Origin creatures.*

There was a nudge at his paw.

"Thank you Dotty," said the little creature to the impatiently tapping grey ferret.

With a quick bow and wave of her hat she was gone, down the postal tube, off to deliver to the other residents. The kedi put the paper down and looked out across the sea of clouds bathed in a generous golden glow. The morning train was picking up its passengers for the day before crossing the mists to the edge of the Twilight. Perhaps it would bring some new guests back with it tonight. This was a rather exciting thought and the little creature's long fluffy tail gave a little wiggle. You see dear reader, new guests bring new stories. The little creature liked stories.

"Yes," said the little one, "the worlds come to me. The Twilight World is the in between, the safe space. And I, the Butler of the great Iskelet Kral, will provide the most peaceful place for a creature's head to rest."

With the slight sound of clinking metal, the kedi named Butler marched towards the door and swung it open to reveal his morning's trials.

Looking out across the darkness, Butler could see the feint outline of a living path wriggling its way through stubbornly. The little kedi stepped out onto the snaking path and took one brave step after another feeling the eyes on his neck. He was smiling. He liked the morning games. In fact, Butler woke up extra early most days to feel the thrill to his very tippy toes with no worries of a silly little thing called time. He kept the door open of course as there is nothing as foolish as shutting oneself in an expanse of moving shadows. The darkness whispered and pulled him forward playfully. He kept his arms stretched out in front so as not to bruise his poor little nose on any hiding walls. Something cold and soft was falling from where the ceiling ought to have been.

With a swirling breeze of laughter, the shadows painted the emptiness with a warm glow. With the comforting flickers of amber, Butler found that he was standing above an expanse of untouched white. Laughing the kedi began to dance with his arms up high to catch the falling white fragments. "Snow!"

The snaking path of shadows became a blazing streak of living fire that laughed alongside him, forming a ring of song. "Hello friends," he said touching the embers for the smallest of moments as they waved their greetings and goodbyes.

Butler watched them, falling towards the ever closer land of perfect white, gritting his smile in petrified excitement. He narrowed his eyes in concentration and there, between the amber and the white, he could still see the comforting open doorway and the golden morning glow of the Twilight. With the falling snow riding the air beside him, the kedi reached out to the door and felt the thud of his own bottom on something soft. Blinking, Butler found himself on top of a pile of laundry awaiting attention. He must have tumbled down the laundry chute. "How splendid!" he exclaimed removing the sock from his tufted ear.

Hopping through the door, Butler thought to peek out of the window and sure enough, the sign swung proudly like any other day. On it was an engraving of a funny looking thing and the words Hostel to Another World. Butler always thought that having a creature of Origin adorning their doorway was rather fitting. With a deep breath, he walked to the centre of the still rather gloomy looking room. With outstretched paws and a heart full of joy the kedi called to the hearth. "Let there be lights in the name of the Master and the King of old. Let them serve as signs to make uprisings and let them give light to this grey world of mine."

He clapped his paws together and the little embers feigning sleep awoke in a blaze as the walls creaked. "Children of Light," spoke Butler softly to the little flames, "if you would."

The kedi quickly ducked and hid himself away as they laughed and did their best to catch him on their way to their lamps. "Really now," muttered Butler patting his singed tail, "you really did get me there. I've not even had my morning coffee yet."

The lamps hopped happily on their polished gloved hands with their magical companions now bathing the room in a soft glow. Butler watched as the remaining Children of Light danced a little last show of magic before settling down to discuss the paper that they had been fed in that morning's delivery. The kedi crawled out from behind the table he'd accidentally overturned and set it perfectly aligned once more. Grumbling, he started busying himself behind the bar and the room was filled with the simple smell of the morning's coffee. As Butler stood wondering why there were two mugs already laid out, he heard the scrape of a stool on the wooden floorboards. "Welcome to the Hostel to Another World," he began, turning to see who might have come to visit him so early in the day.

"A boy blessed with the features of the Origin creature named the cat. You must be Butler," said the visitor. "You're a lot smaller than last I saw you. I suppose this means we're meeting for the first time. The pleasure's all mine."

It was only a little taller than Butler and had funny looking garments draped over its skin. At the very top of it there grew white fur. It sighed a little as it placed itself on a stool, greeting the lamp as an old friend. As the little kedi opened his eyes wide to his new guest he became all a flutter and knocked a mug off the counter in surprise.

"A hooman!"

Three

A Hooman!

"Hello Butler," said the hooman but the little creature was far too busy clearing the broken fragments of china that at first, all that could be heard were the feint murmurings of the Children of Light who were utterly delighted by this turn of events.

The hooman held back a childish little laugh as she took a glance around the room, careful not to move too quickly so as not to petrify the little creature any more than necessary. The hostel was unusually tidy and empty, as if it had not been frequented in weeks. There was an old man who sat in the very corner of the room with a golden teapot next to a familiar stuffed wildcat. It perched rather stoically in its old glass case. The hooman was rather fond of it actually. The wildcat was one of the first things she had noticed in the hostel all those years ago. It was never fussed over. It simply stood there, as if frozen in time, snarling at any unsuspecting travellers. There were other delightful decorations dotted around unsuspectingly of course, including the stuffed crows right above her head, with their precariously draped fairy lights. The hooman noticed the absence of shuffling and looked back towards her rather young old companion. The little creature had stopped entirely. Butler muttered to himself for a moment before turning swiftly on his heals and bowing his head slightly.

"Hello Butler," said the hooman once more.

"Good morning dear visiter," replied the kedi. "Please forgive my rudeness and tardiness in your welcome. Forgive me, am I right in thinking that you are a, well, that you are in fact a hooman?"

"One could say so," said the hooman softly.

"A hooman, a hooman," muttered Butler. "Splendid, splendid," he continued as he fussed under the bar avoiding her gaze. "Let me introduce myself properly. I am your host and guide today Miss Hooman. My name is Butler as you say. I'm very happy that I may be known and called upon even by a Topsider such as yourself. Yes, splendid. Welcome Miss Hooman, welcome to the hostel, the Hostel to Another World."

"The pleasure's all mine Mr Butler," replied the hooman with a bemused smile. "I Chise entrust myself into your care."

The little creature shuffled and avoided her gaze. There was a clink of teapot on teacup from behind and a slight breeze on their cheeks. After a small pause, Chise leaned in as if to tell Butler a secret. "Would you like to hear a story?" she asked to which the little creature couldn't contain a little hop. "I thought you might," she said with a twinkle in her gaze. "You're a hero in this story too you know although you'll have to be patient. The best is always served last and is always, always to be remembered."

With a shuffle, the hooman made herself comfortable in a nearby armchair with pink ruffles while Butler scurried on over with two fresh floral teacups of coffee. He hesitated and with a hop, the kedi scurried on back to bring over a serving of the hostel's special biscuit delights. The two strangers and dear old friends made themselves quite at home and the Children of Light hushed each other expectantly waiting for their story to begin.

"I will tell you the very first adventure story I ever lived. It's a very precious story. One that brought me out of my grey cowardly world and into the worlds of magic. You see, I was a very ordinary little child of no notable talents but I did like to let my mind wander to the edges of imagination. I spent many a day drawing from the limits of that imagination gifted to me. I daresay, the Skeleton King may have took pity on my poor tired soul and led me into the magic all those years ago.

I remember it was a very hot dry day and it made me feel even more sleepy and tiresome. As I walked sluggishly thinking of any possible creature I could sketch for an inkling of excitement I saw a curious thing indeed. There was a very large and round rabbit with great long ears running close by as if late for an appointment. He was more curious still with markings looking remarkably like an unzipped jacket and a strong face with what could easily have been a pirates eyepatch. This caught my attention rather easily of course and I suddenly found myself running after the fluffball. Burning with curiosity, I ran across the little bridge after it, just in time to see it dart past a hedge and through a peculiarly small weathered archway. The archway was longer than I had originally thought of course and went on for some way, shooting suddenly down. It shot down so suddenly in fact that I found myself loosing sight of the tufted tail and I slipped! I fell, fell, fell, gliding through into a shining light. In all my excitement I really didn't think to stop and consider how I would like to get out again so as not to be late for tea time. That would be too much to expect of my child self I suppose.

Thump! There I was, standing quite unharmed by the side of an overgrown archway in the dusk. Time is a rather peculiar thing don't you think? It never seems to behave! I remember, I felt something rise up through my very fingertips and tippytoes. I'm sure you don't even notice it as a magical creature but it was a very new sensation for me. It was the feeling of magic.

I remember I laughed and hurried on forwards a little trying to catch sight of my furry friend again but I sadly found myself to be quite alone. The forest was dense this side of the gate. The trees rustled and whispered to one another as if feasting their gaze on me. Even the wind made me shiver as it rushed past, trying to pull me in. There was an old stone staircase winding upwards past where I could see. I thought to myself that perhaps the rabbit had taken the stairs to his appointment and had simply not been able to spare a moment to wait for me. He did look like a very busy rabbit after all. This is when things got very serious Butler, you had better put the biscuit down for this one. The archway disappeared. It was gone. Poof! Nothing! In its stead there stood two statues that looked older than time itself. The first took the form of Kral the Skeleton King, crowned and regal. The second was of Kurbaga, larger than the first, but missing his head. He sat within a goblet with strange flowing garments, captured forever in the stone.

To make matters even worse, my shadow had started feeling awfully heavy. So, I looked down, and that's when I saw them. The shadows were moving and forming around a skeletal hand. Little shadows buzzed around the bones laughing. The shadows were little children, all swarming in a frenzy around the bones. The hand lurched suddenly. It grabbed my ankle painfully as the head and second arm started wriggling through. The Children of Shadows became even more excited at this and almost completely covered the skeletal creature in a robe of black. I screamed. I wriggled. I kicked. It was exceptionally frightful. The creature slid out of the hole of darkness and crawled closer and closer.

As I closed my eyes to the shapeless face peering down at me, I remember I heard a soft voice on the air. It said, 'Chise? Chise? Where are you, Chise?'

A warm light hit my eyelids and they shone burning amber. I bravely opened my eyes to peak at the morning light that had started to rise. It truly was wonderful. It looked as if the whole world had been painted in a generous helping of golden amber paints. I was a little busy to appreciate it of course. As the skeleton body laughed and mocked me, I kicked one final time, swinging my bag for good measure. The creature let go for a second in bewilderment, sniffing at the backpack inquisitively. This was my chance and I ran with the wind up the inviting staircase, up, up, up! I heard the voice that felt like home calling me again. The skeleton was following, clumsily, gaining speed as it grew accustomed to its flailing limbs. The trees started breaking away, letting the golden hour shine its warmth on my face and on the monster that sought to devour me. I ran blindly, brushing my eyes with my sleeve, hardly aware that the world around me was now falling away into the blanket of clouds. I came to the end of that staircase Butler. There was nowhere else for me left to go but off the very edge into the unknown. The monster was behind me and I heard my name as clear as day riding the wind from on top of that floating staircase in the sky. So I jumped! Would you believe it? I felt him coming for me. That voice was all I needed. I fell right into him. In that moment it was as if time stood still and all the fear had vanished. I was home. They say there is no fear in love, that love casts out fear. Yes, the word eluded me for so very long. Have you ever been in love Butler?" asked the hooman suddenly, to which Butler understandably began coughing the tea he had just taken in.

He shook his head to show that he hadn't come across such a thing as love as he steadied his cough and took a soothing extra large sip of tea. "I suppose not yet," smiled Chise knowingly before continuing. "Well Butler, let me tell you about a little thing called love. Love is a little bit like the magic you hold onto now but one day you will see that it is in fact so much more. Love is patient. Love is kind. It does not insist on going its own way. Love bears all things, believes all things, hopes all things, endures all things. Love came for me when I was lost as I fell helplessly with nothing to my name. It called my name. It gave magic to that name. He carried me and fought my fear, all with that smile. I watched as the skeleton disappeared and faded into the dazzling white light. The Children of Shadows hid themselves from that light, as if ashamed in front of it. He then spoke some unfamiliar words that echoed along the howling winds and those children were reborn to their true selves, filling the winds with bright embers. They were once again, the Children of Light, the magic of the worlds," Chise paused and smiled adoringly at the lamp hopping beside her with the shouts and cheers from the children in the flames before continuing. "And this is where love had to let me go before it came for me again. With a last whisper of a blessing, he dropped me onto the wind and bid it carry me to the first chapter of my new story. I didn't want to leave him but

I somehow knew that I would see him again. I had faith that he would find me, no matter where I fell.

I saw it coming. A little house in the middle of the endless sky. Its little chimney was giving off peaceful white mists and a little train was crossing over the clouds towards it. I came closer and closer and that's when a little creature came to the door, poking his button nose up to the sky as if to welcome me. I floated on the wind into his outstretched arms that were welcoming me to my new home and to my new life in another world."

The Children of Light clapped for Butler who hopped up proudly to take a few delighted bows. "That was me! The wind brought the hooman safely to me!" he squeaked completely forgetting his earlier reaction to a hooman visit. "Splendid! What a story! Is any of it true?"

"Those who have faith and do not doubt can live even greater things. All things are possible," replied Chise with laughing eyes taking a very well deserved chug of tea.

There was a content pause as a pleasant breeze brushed their cheeks.

Butler cleared his throat, "May I ask, Miss Hooman?"

"Ask away old friend," replied Chise happily.

Butler sat down properly in his chair and took a little nibble of a biscuit looking here and there.

"Why is there a hole in my wall?" he asked sheepishly, watching the footsteps as there came a gentle swish of magic. "Oh, hello Cian," said the kedi helplessly as Chise felt a young hand place itself on her shoulder, accompanied by the sound of a clinking teapot.

Four

The Magician's Teapot

Chise peered behind at the gentleman with bemusement. "I was wondering where you were hiding."

The old man from the corner had made some quite considerable adjustments to become a tall young fellow in dashing attire. He lavished a pale green suit completed with a matching bowtie and loafers. He brushed his fair hair from his spectacles and grinned wide, pleased at his successful little party trick.

"Surprised?" asked Cian teasingly.

"Unusual for you to bring company Cian. Do join us," replied Butler gesturing. "Forgive my rudeness, but why did you bring a Topsider to the Twilight? How do you know Miss Hooman?"

"I am a complete stranger," lied Chise firmly.

Cian laughed, "What a cold old woman you are! As for your very sensible question dear Butler, number 1, she bullied me. Number 2, why not? It's the least I can do to shrug off all the unwanted attention. I can't have the Emperor thinking well of me now can I? Not with all his war business on my doorstep. Besides, I'm finding offending the powerful rather fun. Then all I need to do is keep out of their way!"

It seemed a rather silly way to avoid working, but Butler had re-solved long ago that magicians must have a very different pair of brains compared to an ordinary little creature like him. He sighed heavily. Chise carefully placed her teacup down and rested her hooman paw on Butler's arm gently.

With drooping ears Butler asked a question hiding a multitude, "Does there really have to be a war?"

Cian gave a wave of his hand, "A time to love, a time to hate. A time for war and a time for peace. History tends to repeat itself. You'd think we'd learn!" he laughed. "What's wrong?" asked the Magician furrowing his brow.

Butler had suddenly become stiff and had broken out into an alarming cold sweat. He remembered. His eyes shot wide and he darted to lock the hostel door. "Steady on there chap," said Cian standing in concern.

"Butler?" asked Chise calmly.

"You have to leave," choked Butler catching his breath. "Now. Go. Go through the hole you made in my wall!"

It was then that the three unlikely friends heard the firm knocking on the hostel door and a shout, "Open the door, this is the Skeleton Guard responding to your summon!"

"I'm sorry," whispered Butler with wet eyes firmly turned to the ground.

Chise got up from the armchair with the help of Cian and walked slowly towards the little kedi. Butler stood like a statue, frozen, not knowing where to turn as the second set of knocks and shouts came from behind his door. He felt her warm hooman paw on his shoulder and the first drops began to fall from his eyes.

Chise spoke, "It's okay Butler. You were just scared weren't you?"

With a nod, Butler let his face be embraced by both hooman paws. "Leave this to us. Don't you worry about a thing. You go ahead and make me a slice of your famous angel cake next time, how's that?" she asked smiling as Butler's lips curled up slightly. "Right, rebellious magician!"

"Present," replied Cian saluting.

"Don't you think this would be the perfect time to have your fun?" she cooed.

With an evil smile and eyes glinting, the Magician clicked his fingers. Butler watched nervously as the room obediently began to fill with a pleasant darkness of magic, dancing within the lights, echoed by the soft whispers of children. The whispers grew to a beating of chants that hung heavily, pouring out from the embers. The Children of Light always welcomed a magician's mischief.

"I thank you Sir Butler, Miss Hooman, for the opportunity," replied Cian slowly, savouring the words. "Miss Hooman, if you would, please step inside my teapot."

"I thought you'd never ask," replied Chise delighted and with a bold toe step into the small opening she squealed, "In I pop!"

Pop pop pop went the teapot welcoming her in joyfully. With fear turning to excitement, Butler ran up to take a look and noticed there were in fact two in the teapot. The second coiled and purred as the little hooman stroked it behind the ears.

"What's the black fluffy one Mr Cian? Is it from Topside?" he asked wiping his eyes with his sleeve and smiling.

The Magician strode over beaming, "Not at all. I daresay, Fluffy would give a right old fright to most Topsiders," he said raising an eyebrow at the little hooman now hugging the creature. "She's my secret little helper," he whispered to Butler winking.

The door of the hostel flew open then with a crash and a groan, followed by five well presented if slightly exasperated skeleton soldiers. The long flowing black and red coats with embroidered traditional gold patterns befitted the skeletons well, both hiding unnecessary bones and highlighting their stature. They had drawn their small swords ready for combat in the enclosed space.

"What is the nature of the summons and why the locked door?" calmly asked the first skeleton looking from the Magician to Butler still crouched next to the teapot. "Why is there a giant hole in the wall?" he added frowning.

The Magician replied playfully as he bent down, "I was simply stopping by for a light breakfast and decided to invite my little friend who hasn't quite mastered her breaks," he smiled shyly to Butler before a more sinister look crossed his face. "I'd like you to convey a message to the Emperor for me if you would. I'm going to be indisposed for the foreseeable future and I'm not looking for a pen pal. To make sure I'm quite understood, I think it's time I let Fluffy come out for a proper friendly greeting."

The Magician picked the creature carefully out of the teapot, replacing the lid diligently. The Children of Light flared in all corners of the room with dark menacing flames, laughing eerily at the imminent chaos. To the sound of giggles, Cian placed the creature lovingly in front of the boney visitors. "Say hello to my fluffy little friend!"

The creature popped and squeaked bigger and larger than an indoors space should allow. Fluffy was anything but little! Her wide Cheshire grin with all those teeth left one wondering about the friend part as well.

"The hole in the wall makes sense now," muttered Butler as he stood and watched, rather enjoying the spectacle.

As the kedi stared on at the now coiling creature with its cat shaped face and larger than life eyes, he had to admit that she was indeed very fluffy. In fact, the creature's black fur was truly magnificent. It positively glistened in the glow cast by the dancing Children of Light. This would have been a rather beautiful moment, meeting a rare creature, were it not for the imminent chaos and swift cleaning thereafter.

As Cian welcomed Fluffy out with a chin ruffle he grinned and proclaimed, "Escape for your life. Do not look back or stop anywhere in the valleys of the Twilight. Escape to the horizon, lest you be swept away and devoured!"

The skeletons saw that the moment had come when they must in fact do something. While they rustled themselves into formation and out of a panic, Fluffy opened her mouth to welcome the first skeleton. The poor soul would soon have been very much nibbled, however, at that very moment, the skeletons threw a handy net around Fluffy's neck, accidentally saving their companion. The net caught the creature surprisingly well and the thrashing and gnashing began. After that, there was a great deal of commotion in the hostel, and a whole lot of future cleaning for our dear friend Butler. In fact, the skeletons had quite forgotten who they had come to arrest. They did not see Butler crawling to the hole in the wall with the teapot. They did not see the Magician who was happily sending objects flying at their shins.

"Where are all these flying stools coming from?" shouted a skeleton indignantly as he attempted to pry Fluffy's dripping jaw off his comrade.

The Magician was quite in his element, spouting magic from the countless corners of the room, hiding in the smoke and moving in the squeals and bangs, laughing all the way. By the cover of madness, Cian soon slipped away in the form of a golden ferret to the see through pipes of the delivery routes. He thought it rather a marvellous idea to lead the noisy skeletons away from his favourite drinks behind the bar. He aimed some more forks and knives at them as Fluffy coiled herself around the unlucky one. Appearing to be dancing among the rafters, the golden ferret began to sing a song to infuriate the skeletons further.

This is what he sang:

The dead come only to steal and kill and destroy
I have come that they may have life
Let all who have life
Have life in the full!

He sang to his heart's content and flung some more bits of furniture for good measure as a flurry of tiny little footsteps could be heard going a *pitter patter* from above their heads. Almost all the skeletons came after the four legged creature wiggling his bum, with one left to be nibbled by Fluffy. Some shouted and waved their swords at the ceiling and others raced along the tables. One kind soul returned to persuade the giant cat snake to let their friend go with a tasty looking fruitcake in hand. They were all awfully angry of course. I daresay, no one likes to be called dead, let alone be accused of stealing. With their colourful silky garments now covered in dust, they looked ready to just about give up.

"Oh come now, that simply won't do," said Cian whistling one last encouraging charm.

The hostel's pipes were full of excited little feet. To the room's astonishment, the postal brigade burst through and began to dart around, taunting the skeletons with each and every jump. The ferrets had never been particularly polite creatures although they did try awfully hard when on the clock. The golden ferret under the cover of yet more ferrets darted towards the hole in the wall. "Time to scram girl!" he whistled.

Fluffy uncoiled, carefully opening its mouth to accept the cake from the skeleton soldier, and at the speed of lightning bolted towards the train tracks in the clouds. Butler pushed himself away from the wall and hugged the teapot tight, peaking through his elbow as he watched a flurry of ferrets descend the side of the hostel to accompany the Magician's whim of an idea. They were swiftly followed of course by the skeletons, shouting carelessly that they were all under arrest.

Butler watched amused as the giant cat snake and the army of ferrets soared above the clouds, followed poorly by a handful of jogging skeletons. The Magician rode Fluffy like a dragon, following the tracks to the edge of the Twilight where he would undoubtedly slip through the gate to Topside where no creature with even half a brain would dare follow.

A stillness came over the Hostel to Another World as the Children of Light finished the last of their dark magic breakfast. Butler got up to help the last two skeletons leave, somewhat hobbling, and they shook his hand handing over a generous number of coins for damages caused by their inept handling of the morning's summon. Butler thanked them warmly, pocketing the gift, bowing to see them out.

After he was quite alone, the kedi sat down in the only not upturned armchair to get over all the excitement. He looked about himself with great long sighs and started entertaining the thought of simply banning the Magician temporarily. Butler then began to wonder what had become of the hooman in the teapot. He hopped up and scurried on over. With a quick glance around, he lifted the lid only to discover a very ordinary little teapot, with no magic, no creatures, and certainly no hoomans.

Five

The Skeleton Banquet

Covered in dust, having just repaired and pretend repaired all that had been broken or thrown that morning, Butler found himself in the presence of Sir Raven, messenger to the Prince of Skeletons. Prince Béla had decided to place a last minute booking, the cheek. Thus, Butler found himself running around his makeshift dining hall with a hurriedly assembled set of hired skeleton waiters in tuxedos. His all black tuxedo with its subtly adorned characters had been presented to him rather ceremoniously only an hour before the skeleton banquet, and so he was trying rather hard not to trip on his own trouser legs.

While Prince Béla was drinking his banana wine, he was struck by what he believed to be a splendid idea. He gave orders to bring the golden engraved goblets that Nazar his father had taken from Kurbaga's Central Church, so that he, his nobles, and his soldiers could drink from them and praise the Skeleton King. As the party continued in full swing with refills of banana wine at the ready, there was a firm knock at the door. The delivery skeletons walked in rigidly, trying their hardest to look ceremonious as they walked past the thing in the shadows that tried to swipe at their shins. After an awkward bow to their Prince, the goblets were distributed like trophies to all who were present. As the delivery skeletons gratefully took their leave, the thing in the shadows snapped and growled at them for a second time. Butler had told the Prince's men numerous times that pets were not allowed, a rule he had especially designed because of them, but to his disappointment it had landed on deaf invisible ears.

The kedi hopped away from the snarling thing in the shadows and as he went to present the last goblet he found himself being thrown down onto a bench. "Join us boy," said the owner of the skeletal hand which proceeded to swipe the goblet. "I'll have that one. Leave the rest to the tuxes," he said gruffly. "Tell me boy, I heard you were attacked by that magician Cian this morning and you had to use your secret button. That's awfully rough," he said feigning concern. "I trust my men dealt with him for you?"

"As swiftly as the fish fly," lied Butler routinely. "Thank you for your service and continued patronage," he said bowing his head respectfully.

The Prince waved his hand and poured Butler a drink. "No need for any of that. We're all friends here and your hostel is about the only place both my nobles and my soldiers can agree upon. Tell me boy, ever since that magician agreed to be enlisted he's been hiding with the cockroaches. Haven't been able to catch him since."

Butler could think of but only one thing to do and that was to help Cian weasel, or perhaps, ferret out of what was likely his very own fault. "He lied. He did that to play you. He's always making empty promises and then running away from them Sir, Prince, Béla."

"And he hopes to weasel out of a war that has both the World Beneath and the World Above squabbling like little rats in front of a juicy piece of blue cheese?" asked the Prince with a serious face.

Butler's mind ran through a series of unhelpful comments before managing to offer an apology and a glory to the World Beneath. The kedi thought hard and carefully continued, "He's a real troublemaker your Highness. He really would be no good in a war. All he's capable of is destroying all my furniture."

"He is unusual," the Prince agreed with a hearty laugh. "But I did instruct him that I'd grant any wish within reason and enough gold to fill all his daft loafers if he agreed to defend his homeland. I counted 59 last I visited."

"59 Sir?" asked Butler.

"Loafers," replied the Prince, painfully clamping his skeleton companion's mouth shut before there could be any interruption. "There were 29 and a bit pairs of them all lined up on display in his hallway."

"He does enjoy nice things," agreed Butler who couldn't help shift uncomfortably and do a little ponder. *Why did the Prince count the Magician's loafers?* He shook his little fluffy face and dutifully continued. "Surprisingly he doesn't care about money. Half the time he doesn't seem to care what happens to anyone or anything as long as he gets his way. He's helpful when it suits him. He disappears when things get bad."

The Prince was smiling, "Thank you boy," he said. "Your honesty has put me at ease. I had heard that he was someone who did anything for money, living to flaunt his wealth and power. You've shown me how very wrong my assumptions have been. He's just the magician our world needs."

"Drat!" Butler exclaimed unexpectedly. "He told me to tell you that he's nothing of the sort!"

"He did, did he?" smiled Prince Béla satisfied, bringing his face dangerously close. "I'd like you to convey a little message to that pesky magician if you would my boy. We need to reclaim the World Beneath East and reunite it with the West. This isn't fun and games for any of us. It's our home and our brothers and sisters. We will not let the Topsiders do as they please," he said leaving a dramatic pause. "I am appointing Cian the Kingdom's Magician as of now, with the Prince's command to join the front lines. Before the year is out, with the Magician on our side we will win this war and the Topsiders will be put in their place!"

There was un uproar of cheering, banging of bony fists, and stomping of armoured feet as the banquet was filled with the shouts of skeletons. Not unusual behaviour of course, but still a touch too noisy for Butler's little tufted ears that he swiftly clamped in his paws. *Why do skeletons have to be so dramatic?*

There came a sudden hushed quiet. Far too sudden for comfort. Even the clinking and munching from the thing in the shadows had ceased. Butler opened his eyes and ears and looked about himself, stopping at his roughly mended wall where all gazes were affixed. The fingers of a hooman paw had appeared and had started writing on the fake wallpaper near the lamp stand. The lamp was slowly edging away on its white glove, which was an understandable and smart response. Prince Bêla watched the hooman paw as it wrote with gaping jaw and shivering bones. After the paw had quite finished its job, it waved a rather rude goodbye and evaporated, leaving the message to its unhappy audience.

The Prince summoned all the enchanters, magicians, and diviners that he could remember. He towered over the wise creatures of the World Beneath and announced, "Whoever reads this writing and tells me what it means will be clothed in a purple robe, their boots will be filled with gold, and they will be made the third highest adviser in my court."

The wise creatures obliged and spoke with one another, debating aimlessly, but none of them could read the writing or tell the Prince what it meant. At this, Prince Bêla became even more terrified and his bones became even more fidgety. His advisers were baffled.

Upon hearing the conversations of the Prince and his advisers, Butler could not keep quiet any longer. "Your Highness. May the Prince live forever," he said. "Do not be alarmed. There is someone in your kingdom who has the spirits of the Children of Light in him. He is the royal cupbearer to the Prince and a devout disciple of the Holy Church. He has a keen mind, knowledge and understanding, and also the ability to interpret dreams, explain riddles, and solve difficult problems. Call for Tovey of the Priesthood, and he will tell you what the writing means," said Butler stiff lipped, bowing his head with pounding chest.

"Tovey?" asked Prince Bêla thinking hard.

"You called?" came a low gruff voice from the end of the table. All eyes shot towards the owner of that voice. "It's been a while Butler," said the cloaked figure, pushing off his hood with a giant fluffy white paw to reveal two very long fluffy white ears and a set of drooping whiskers. "You're looking well," he said bowing his head slightly.

Butler squeaked and crimson creeped along his ears. *Squeak? Why did you squeak? You're a kedi, a descendent of the Origin creature the cat.* Butler's thoughts raced as he avoided Tovey's intense gaze, choosing to stare at his polished oversized dress shoes. Whispers rippled through the room.

Isn't that the Magic Rabbit of the Holy Priesthood? Why is he so tall? Isn't he the one who's been whispering in the High Priest's ear lately? I heard he flattened a whole village in the East. Isn't that his homeland?

"Silence!" roared the Prince through the dim giving Butler such a fright that the poor little creature almost fell off the bench in surprise.

The Prince addressed Tovey the Magic Rabbit, "Are you one of the exiles my father the late Prince brought from the East? Is it true that the spirits of the Children of Light are in you?" he asked and then continued without waiting for a response. "If you can read this writing and tell me what it means, you will be clothed in the royal purple robes, I will fill your boots with gold, and I will set you to be my third highest advisor to serve my kingdom."

Tovey and Butler's eyes met for a moment before Butler swiftly looked away.

The Magic Rabbit stepped out from the bench and began walking towards the wall, answering the Prince with his back, "You may keep your gifts for yourself and give your rewards to someone else. Nevertheless, I will read the writing for the Prince and tell him what it means. Your Princeship, our creator Kurbaga gave your father Nazar sovereignty and greatness and splendour. Because of the high position he gave him, all the worlds and creatures of every language dreaded and feared him. Those the late Prince wanted to put to death, he put to death. Those he wanted to spare, he spared. But when his heart became arrogant and hardened with pride, he was deposed from his royal throne and stripped of his glory. He was driven away from his royal palace and given the mind of a Topsider creature. He lived with the so called wild asses and ate grass! His body was drenched with the dew of the Tree of Life until he acknowledged that the Most High Master is sovereign over all nations and all worlds, setting over them anyone he wishes.

But you, Prince Bêla, have not humbled yourself, though you knew all this. Instead, you have set yourself up against the Master. You had the goblets from his temple brought to you, and you and your nobles, and your soldiers drank wine from them. You praised the Skeleton King - Iskelet Kral, who sleeps in the ground, repenting for eternity for his disobedience.

You have dedicated your life to bring dishonour and contempt to Kurbaga, who even the Skeleton King sought to please. The Master holds in his hands your life and all your ways and yet you never see, you never listen, and you have never called out his name on your invisible tongue. Therefore, he has sent the despised hooman paw that wrote the inscription.

The inscription written reads:
MENE, MENE, TEKEL, PARSIN

Here is what these words mean:
Mene: Kurbaga has numbered the days of your attempt at leadership and brought it to an end.
Tekel: You have been weighed on the bubble scales of judgement and found sorely wanting.
Parsin: Your world is divided and foreigners will come to claim it for themselves.

Your end has come Prince Bêla of the Skeleton Guard."

As if waiting for the dramatic effect, an ominous winged shadow clumsily landed on the open window frame. The room watched as its skeletal claw started biting into the wood for balance, adding once again to Butler's monthly repairs bill.

"It's the Angel of Death!" came a shout.

"The reaper's here!" came another.

There was a mad rush towards the hostel door as the defenders of the World Beneath pushed their comrades out of the way in a blind panic.

Butler peeped from under the table at the creature in the window, "Oh it's you!" exclaimed the little creature happily amongst the ruckus of panicking flailing skeletons.

To the astonishment of the terrified trained fighters, the little kedi hopped up, quickly grabbing a lollipop jar, and skipped over to the window. With a great big smile on his tiny little face, he held out a lollipop with his long stripy tail and said, "It's lemon today!"

Six

The Angel of Death

The Angel of Death sat at the window with skeletal wings folded for convenience. The light of the forever morning sun bathed its snow white skin and there was a pleasant fluttering of a breeze which came from above the sea of crimson clouds beneath. The creature had a simple black mask attached to it, covering its jaw like a muzzle. If any of the skeletons had a shred of bravery left, they were surely regretting it now, for when any thought to try and look at the face of their reaper, from behind those fashionable white locks they would catch a glimpse of the creature's royal, overwhelming gaze. Those brave souls found that they simply must look away or surely die. Although the room was filled with the sound of trembling bones, it was a curious feeling. The skeletons a moment ago had thrown themselves towards the door and would have done just about anything to leave that scene to their upcoming nightmares. Yet now, now that they felt those regal eyes, they dared not go. The Angel of Death crouched in the window frame, waiting patiently as the skeletons crowded themselves around the tables in the shape of a half-coliseum. The room watched in astonishment as the formally timid little kedi skipped over to the thing in the window brandishing a lollipop instead of a sword.

With a great big smile the little one exclaimed, "It's lemon today! I hope you like it!"

The long stripy tail reached forwards towards the Angel of Death with a bright yellow lollipop. As the kedi waited, careful not to scare the creature away, the thing in the window reached out its non-skeletal hand. This was all very usual protocol for Butler of course. *Why are skeletons always so dramatic? What's that?* A silver thread had glittered on the reaper's wrist for a moment, reaching and searching into the air. Bewildered, Butler felt an utterly unbearable curiosity, although he knew very well that curiosity killed the cat. *Just a little touch can't hurt can it?* With a successfully gifted lollipop, Butler slowly and gently reached out his little paw and touched the silver thread.

Falling? Or maybe rising?

Suddenly, the scene disappeared and the silver thread wrapped it-self around Butler's waist, snaking upwards, winding, unravelling, and intertwining once again. The little kedi squirmed to catch his breath as even the regal eyes left him falling and rising alone.

Tick tick tick.

The clocks hovered calmly around him as he floated, breaking through the shroud of mysterious swirling mists. Some were ticking forwards, others were gleefully running backwards. A flurry of silver threads danced around, thoroughly enjoying themselves. It did look fun. Butler settled his racing thoughts and took heart, vowing to catch at least one silver streak. With an inkling of courage, he reached out his paw and watched as his very own hooman paw caught a flickering thread. A name welled up inside him and he heard a familiar voice cheekily using his personal mouth to shout through the mists. There was a sound of a young girl crying. The teardrops were trickling down his face and he used his hooman paws to wipe them.

"Chise," responded a low gentle voice.

Butler looked around in alarm and saw his paws were rightfully and beautifully his once more.

"Daddy's treasure," came a soft cooing voice as Butler watched the happy faces of what looked to be a family appear around a hooman cub.

Who's that in the window? Can't you see him?

The thoughts of the hooman cub not yet able to roar echoed through the mists as the hoomans around her gave all manners of toys to her outstretched arms.

"I will never be far away Chise," came the same gentle voice and the shadow in the window faded.

There came the painful sensation of a silver thread being cut. The feeling of eternal loss of something or someone who was there from the very beginning now gone. Butler screamed out the pain and fell to the ground with clenched fists. His hands had matured to a woman's. "I will always catch you when you fall," said the voice through the mists. "It's okay Chise. Let me catch you."

These must be Chise's memories.

Butler watched as time passed and the scenes of frustration and pain danced in and out of view.

Why is nothing going right? How much can one hooman endure?

The mother was grieving deeply, over and over again. She had never loved anyone as much as she loved him, and she never will again. Chise was becoming more like him - a blessing and a curse.

Chise was a little girl again. She didn't look like the Chise the little kedi knew. She stood angry. She turned her back on it all. Her body covered in bruises, broken and battered. "Come Chise," echoed the voice invitingly. "Leave that world behind. Come join my world and stay with me."

"Chise don't!" Butler screamed into the nothingness but instead, he felt his own elation and little feet start running towards the voice and the light.

"Chise, you can't go! This world will..."

There came the creeping sound of laughter and Butler felt a childish joy as he ran after a rabbit, leading the way into the light. The silver threads had almost completely intertwined. The light beckoned and a figure stood bathed in the light like an angel.

"I will always come for you," it said holding out its hand.

"Run! Before the silver threads join!" Butler shouted.

His voice couldn't reach. She couldn't notice. The silver threads had gathered like one of the stars of the great skies. "Please don't take her away Sir Angel," said Butler as he stood helplessly watching from a distance.

The ticking clocks became louder once more, ticking out of time with one another. The little kedi watched the angel place a silver thread around the child's tiny wrist.

"Time never did run smoothly for us," it said in a kind and simple hooman voice.

As the thread bound the little hooman cub's arm, the great silver star above exploded, splitting into countless shooting stars that rained across the mists. Butler floated there, gazing at them, at the angel in the light, at the little girl. His racing thoughts escaped into a single word, "Beautiful."

The little girl reached out with a peculiar look on her face, "Butler, run!" she shouted.

The little kedi screamed at the top of his lungs as the silver star fell and engulfed him.

Is it over yet? I really should get back to work you know little silver threads.

Butler felt the blinding light from behind his little paws slowly fade once more. Reluctantly, he lowered them and blinked to take in his new scene. It was not the scene of a skeleton banquet.

Drat! It's that weird angel again.

Butler felt himself blush at his own childishness and swiftly stood up to face the radiant figure in the grey room. The kedi could see clearer now and the white angel looked more peculiar than Butler had expected. He seemed to be bandaged in many places. Even its eyes had been covered, almost as if the bandages were hiding something.

The blindfolded angel walked away from Butler towards the windowpane which vanished from his hidden gaze. With every step he took there sprung and withered wildflowers of every colour, joyously living and dutifully dying in a mere instant. With each step closer the windowpane widened to give the angel the best possible view.

Must be convenient being an angel.

The white cloaked figure beckoned Butler to approach with a carefully bandaged right hand. Within two metres of each other, the angel signalled, warning Butler to come no closer. Butler stopped short and felt a chill run down his fur as the noises became entangled on the air.

Confused lamenting moans were floating on the winds towards Butler's twitching ears. They welled up inside Butler's chest and a sense of loss and regret pounded at his soul. The white figure watched and listened as if in thought before looking over at Butler and floating out into the bleak grey beyond the window. Butler carefully pulled his body over to the open window unable to hide his curiosity. Of course after looking out, he almost wished he hadn't. The mist was filled with empty wandering souls, moaning in anguish as they dragged their legs forwards. Each and every one of them wore chains that bore heavy around their ankles and weighed on their souls. Looking down at his own chained ankles he felt a pinch of anger. Butler was familiar with these chains.

Why did you have to betray me?

He held his chest and took a deep breath before looking bravely out to the idly floating angel.

"Why are you showing me this? Don't you think I regret it all enough as it is?" he shouted out to it.

The angel stayed silent.

This made Butler even more angry, "If he hadn't let them take me. If he hadn't left. If he, if he," Butler's words ached and he knew he didn't want to continue. "Just take me back. I've had enough."

The angel remained silent.

Butler looked down at the pitiful sight beneath him. A skeleton soul with chains entangling him was moaning loudest of all, unable to reach out and help what appeared to be his hooman cub. Another lay crying out, unable to reach an older hooman woman holding a photo. They wanted to help. They wanted to do the right thing and their chains were forever holding them back. They'd lost their last chance.

"The saddest thing about betrayal is that it never comes from your enemies," said the angel thoughtfully through the haze.

Butler looked over to it in surprise and the angel continued, "I have seen all the things that are done under the sun. All of them are meaningless, a chasing after the wind. That is, all the things done not from the heart."

"What do you mean from the heart?" called the kedi over the noise.

The angel smiled for the first time and opened its arms wide as if ready to embrace, "What do you want to do?"

Butler held tightly to the windowpane and thought about it. *What do I want? Why is that such a hard question?*

He looked down at the wandering souls and replied, "I don't want to become like them," he said pointing.

The angel clicked its fingers and appeared much too close to Butler's little face, "What do you want?" it repeated.

Butler looked down at his ankles covered in rusted chains and said the words that he thought he'd never say. They made him feel rather silly in fact.

"Your chains are not as strong as the one who fights for you," it said with a click and Butler felt a newness of spirit well up inside him. "It's okay to want things," said the angel smiling. "Regrets are heavier than any chains."

With a last click, the angel disappeared into the mists and the souls grew quieter, fading into the shimmering air. The silver threads shone bright once more, darting around the empty space in utter delight. The silver intertwined to one single thread, joining two bright stars that hovered and nestled themselves comfortably into the palms of Butler's outstretched paws. They guided him together and brought the little kedi back down into his own little world, back to the skeleton banquet.

The little kedi blinked. He found himself lying under a comfy officer's coat with no messy ruckus of skeletons, no strange writing on the wall, and certainly no creatures at the windows. There was no mess at all in fact. *How peculiar. Now that really is worrying.*

There was a note next to him:

Dear Butler,

Ever so sorry for what happened earlier. I do hope you'll forgive the Skeleton Guard. As such, I'm leaving a small token of our appreciation with this letter. Do take it and use it in any way you see fit.

I borrowed one of your lollipops to gift the Angel of Death. I hope you don't mind. He was surprisingly well trained and I still have all my fingers!

I didn't tell the others but I saw something Butler, something that may be hard to explain, but I believe you may have seen it too.

The hooman is someone rather important isn't she?

I hope you know what I mean. If not, do ignore my ramblings.

I had my men clean up for you. Being messy is an awfully bad habit of ours but I do think there is hope for change.

Goodness, is that the time already? I must dash.

I trust this letter finds you well dear Butler and thank you again, the banana wine was truly excellent.

Yours faithfully,
Prince Yuki

P.S. Prince Béla is dead.

May the dust return to the ground it once came, as the spirit returns to Kurbaga who gave it life.

P.SS I let the hooman stay. I hope that's alright.

Butler looked up in alarm.

"I suppose I wasn't who you were expecting," said a gruff voice.

Seven

A Topsider's Plot

"Tovey!" shouted Butler dropping the letter.

Just when things couldn't get any more unusual. There he stood, slouching yet still towering over the room. Indeed, Tovey the Magic Rabbit was looking very out of place, not helped by his long ears almost brushing the rafters.

"I'm afraid I have bad news and even worse news. Which would you like to hear first?"

"Hello to you too!" shouted Butler indignantly. "I don't want either. Where's the hooman?"

"Asleep," barked Tovey. "Leave her be. We have more pressing matters."

The kedi raised his brows, "I doubt that somehow."

"Would you listen to me for one minute?" Tovey shouted flailing his fluffy white arms impatiently.

Butler was now pretending to be silently indifferent, tapping away with his foot. "Suit yourself," shrugged the rabbit. "You're so weird. The more pressing of our matter's then, which I'm sure is connected anyway," he said gesturing to the angry red flashing light next to the back door, "is that we're being summoned to Topside. It's been going for half an hour now and it's getting more angry. And don't you even try to say that you're not going or that I'm not going with you!"

That was exactly what Butler wanted to say.

However, this news certainly caught Butler's attention. He had heard of the mythical red light but had never seen it look alive.

The little kedi tilted his head to one side, "You stubborn rabbit. You haven't changed at all," and before Tovey could protest such uncalled for insults, the kedi puffed out his chest, standing as tall as he could muster. "I suppose the time has come to pay a visit to the hoomans of Topside. They seem to be making my hostel their home anyway," he said badly hiding his frustration. "Now I, I will be easily disguising myself as a fellow Topsider."

With a wave of paw, the kedi blurred and shimmered like a mirage on a hot summer's day before settling on the aesthetic of a petite yet handsome hooman man. "You however, Mr Magic Rabbit of the Holy Priesthood, have no magic other than making little paper cranes."

"You think you're so funny don't you?" retorted Tovey catching the little kedi in a headlock.

The rabbit smiled to himself. It was nice to see some of the old Butler again. "Now quit being a goofball and change me into something good too. Make it anything. That angry red light's not going to wait forever. And the Children of Light told me themselves that there's someone we need to meet. It's on our heads if this someone gets tired of waiting and the future of the worlds gets altered."

"Well that sounds serious," replied the kedi thoughtfully.

"That's what I've been trying to tell you!" Tovey boomed. "Now stop playing around and change me into something too. Anything, just make it quick."

"Anything you say?" grinned Butler evilly, weaselling out of the rabbit's grip.

"Just make sure I can still talk you insufferable cat. There's something really important I need to tell you and this mysterious someone," he huffed exhausted. "And make sure the form keeps its magic. Who knows what's waiting for us. I'll let you choose the stupid aesthetic."

"The fancy priest is awfully foul mouthed today." Butler taunted, jumping out of the Magic Rabbit's reach.

"I'm off duty!" he bellowed so that even the Children of Light clamped their non-existent ears.

"Fine! Fine. Stand clear, Mr Off Duty Rabbit," teased Butler waltzing over to the angry red light. "I'll change you as we transfer over. It'll be quicker. Children of Light, are you ready?"

The little children joined together from between their logs in a long slither of amber flame. "As ready as we were last time this happened," one said.

"So not ready at all?" piped up another.

"Look on the bright side, they'll be the ones to die if anything goes wrong, not us," reasoned a third.

"Oh for goodness sake," Butler snapped at them. 'Hold on tight all of you. One, two, three!"

The whole room filled with a strange white fog. Tovey's eyes began searching but it was hard to see clearly. It felt as if the very Twilight had come undone, swirling around them in a sickening spiral. Even the Children of Light seemed serious which was a very bad sign indeed. Tovey clung tighter to the handy small pillar next to him that kept him from falling into the nothingness. He watched wide eyed as Butler easily steadied himself and effortlessly cast the tricky charm. With a whoosh, there was a wave of magic and Tovey locked his eyes firmly shut as the charm hit him in yet more swirling motions. With long steadying breaths, the rabbit repeated Kurbaga's prayer over and over in his mind, imagining his feet on a very ordinary floor in a very ordinary house in the sky.

As if listening, the room slowed and settled to reveal the very same Hostel to Another World with the stuffed wildcat snarling at the window.

"Did it work?" Tovey coughed.

"I should hope so," responded the Children of Light in a whisper from the chimney. "Otherwise we've died and gone to the pits of hell. Look at all your ugly faces."

Butler laughed heartily with joyous relief and hopped around to see what on earth had actually happened. They were not alone, just as the kedi had expected. There behind the familiar bar in pretty waistcoats and mini top hats stood two hoomans.

"You really do just pop up everywhere don't you?" Butler sighed.

"Surprised?" replied Cian delightedly wiping a glass. "Who do you think called you?" the Magician asked with raised eyebrows. "Now to business. This is no time for a chit-chat. Your guest will be here any minute. Dotty please get the gentleman a drink."

"Yes, right away Sir," she said accentuating the Sir teasingly as she prepared Butler's favourite banana wine.

"And for the little cutie fluffball," cooed the Magician, handing over a small bottle that read *Rabbit Juice - A sugar and lactose free treat for your little rascal.*

"Shut up," Tovey mumbled snatching the bottle clumsily with two tiny paws.

"You're lucky we allow pets," added Dotty cheekily as she gestured to the table at the window. "We saved you the best table in the house."

Butler looked past the window at the unfamiliar snowy scene as hoomans occasionally trudged past running their morning errands as quickly as their clumsy limbs would take them. There were no other visitors and the hostel was eerily quiet. In fact, the hoomans passing by didn't seem to pay an ounce of notice at the well-dressed gentleman in the window, or at the very round pet rabbit awkwardly sipping from a glass bottle.

Tovey couldn't help but notice Butler fidgeting. He wanted to say something, words of encouragement perhaps, but the distance had crept in again and he had no idea what he could possible say. So, the handsome gentleman and the fluffy rabbit in his lap sipped their drinks in silence, waiting for the door to swing open. They watched as a hooman came out of a black stylish car. The hooman glanced all round as if afraid someone were watching before powerfully striding towards the hostel door.

"For your date," said Dotty suddenly making Butler jump as she set a drink on the table.

Sure enough, it was at that moment that the door chime jingled and a fleeting cold breeze hit Butler's shins. The kedi took a sip of banana wine without looking as he felt the figure walking over. At the sound of the chair scraping the floorboard, he steadied his resolve and looked up. A tall woman in black business attire and black hair was now removing her matching black shades. It really was all black. Butler decided it safe to assume that this was a Topsider fashion and wondered if his offensively pink shirt might have been the wrong choice. She sat back, mutely and efficiently.

There was an awful silence.

Butler gulped feeling the heat of the wine trickling down his throat.

Finally, the hooman leant in, "Are you Butler of the Hostel to Another World and Tovey the Magic Rabbit of the Holy Priesthood?" she whispered.

"We are," replied Butler leaning away.

"Shh!" hissed the hooman in hushed tones. "Use your secretive voice. It's not safe even here."

"Why, are you afraid of Cian and his helper?" Butler hissed back. "There's no one else here and I assure you, the Magician's an idiot but he's not stupid."

"The Magician and his assistant are meddlesome but no, I'm used to them now. It's the Angel of Death that would betray us to the Skeleton King. He pops up almost as much as that daft magician," she replied leaning closer still. "I'm sure you know who I mean."

"If we're talking about who we trust," said Butler loudly, "how do we know you're a friend?"

"Not meaning to be rude Miss Hooman," added Tovey squeakily, "but as much as I've been instructed to convene on a message with you, we are in fact complete strangers."

"You're very right," sighed the hooman sitting back. "Introductions. My name is Dianna Lions-White but you can call me Die," she smiled in what she hoped was a friendly way. "I have been sent by the Federation of Riland," she whispered again, enunciating. "A country of the hooman world," she added. "I have brought you a gift. It's from the prophecy Mr Tovey."

With these words she took out a small intricate looking hooman weapon named a gun.

Tovey and Butler stared at it in surprise until Tovey broke the silence, "It's really true. Butler, careful touching that thing. It's an Angel Killer."

Butler's hooman paw stopped mid-air and hovered before returning itself to his lap.

"You both have some explaining to do," replied Butler coldly, wondering why everyone around him seemed to be plotting with hoomans.

"That's right," replied Die. "Tovey, I think it's time you took over. Now there's one last thing on my part."

The hooman became quiet and signalled for them to come in closer, "They say that Dawei has started awakening."

At the sound of the foreign name a very curious thing happened. Although Butler had no possibility of knowing who Dawei was, the moment the hooman spoke that name, he felt quite different indeed. Curiosity welled up inside his chest but to his disappointment, the hooman pushed blindly forward, "If you would Mr Tovey."

The Magic Rabbit nodded and finished the last of his Rabbit Juice, climbing up onto the table between them, "Right. So, Kurbaga spoke to me through the Children of Light as I prayed before shutting my eyes last night. I rushed over at once and found that Yuki fellow writing a letter. He ran off as soon as he saw me of course. I don't blame him. I saw a picture in my head of us in the hostel of Topside and," he paused here, "I saw the Angel Killer just as it is now, lying untouched on the table." He stood up tall with his tiny back legs. "There's a prophecy that may change the very course of the worlds." Tovey's eyes glazed over and the Magic Rabbit's priestly voice took over. "This is what I saw:

Gliding on the winged chariot of Kurbaga's angels, I was brought through a cacophony of little spirits and set down in the middle of a valley of bones. Kurbaga paid the charioteers their gifts and weaved a multicoloured coat upon my shoulders. He led me back and forth, and I saw a great many bones, dry and forgotten from the passing of ages.

Kurbaga paused his orb to rest a whisker length away and he asked me, 'Son of Origin, can these bones live?'

I replied, 'Sovereign Master, you alone know.'

He waved his froglike hand and a skeleton cloaked in majestic purple towered next to him.

'Dry bones, hear the words of the Skeleton King! This is what your king says to you:

I will make breath enter you, and you will come to life. I will attach hidden tendons to you and will cover you with magic. I will put breath in you, and then you will know that I am your king.'

There was a noise, a rattling sound, and the bones came together, bone to bone. I watched as the tendons flashed emerald, but there was no breath in them.

As the Skeleton King stood unmoving like a puppet with no commands, Kurbaga decided he trusted me to do the rest. He commanded me, 'Prophesy to the breath. Prophesy, rabbit son of mine. This is what the Skeleton King says:

Come, breath, from the four winds and breathe your magic into these slain, that they may live!'

I prophesied diligently hoping to make my Master proud and the winds took pity on me. As breath entered them, I fell to my knees in horror. The bones came to life and stood far too close for comfort - a vast army.

Then the Master took the spirits and rose up, carried by the winds. I stood and followed the golden bubble with my eyes as it danced across the army of the dead, marvelling at the twinkling of spirits and magic. Kurbaga's voice echoed all around me, calling me to attention, 'Son of Origin, these bones are the people of Origin and this is what they say:

Our bones are dried up and our hope is gone. Why do we live? You should leave us to rot and be forgotten for that is what we deserve.

Therefore prophesy to their tormented spirits. This is what the Skeleton King says:

My people, I am going to open your graves and bring you up from them. I will lead you into the new land of Origin to replace the old, a place where even magic is no longer needed. Then you, my people, will know that I am your king. I will put my spirit in you and you will live.

My servant Dawei will rule over you my people in the new land of Origin, and you will have your peace. You will follow the true king and will be careful to keep my secrets. You will live in the land where your ancestors lived. You and your children and your children's children will live there forever, and Dawei my servant will be your justice. My dwelling place will be with you. I will be your guardian, and you will be my creation. The worlds will know that I Iskelet Kral make the Origins holy, and I will dream among you forever.'"

A skeleton army coming alive and living in the land of Origin? That doesn't bode well for the hoomans. Indeed, it would be rather inconvenient for all the worlds. Butler thought as hard as his little head could muster.

There was an uncomfortable silence.

"Who is Dawei?" asked Butler carefully.

"Dawei?" said Die. "He's a servant of the Skeleton King in scripture. He was put to sleep by Kurbaga for all of eternity in the same way the traitor Skeleton King himself lies at the centre of the earth. But the word has reached even us on Topside that Dawei has started to awaken. And now this prophecy," she waved her hand in dismay.

"He won't turn us into skeletons will he?" asked the kedi.

"Goodness no, that would be manageable!" answered the hooman with a great big laugh. "Turn us into skeletons? No. They will replace the old. Hoomans will be replaced with an army of the dead. Hell, we'll likely all disappear if the skeletons get their way."

Tovey started coming back to his own rabbit self and shook his head hard, letting his ears flop from side to side.

"You had a mysterious skeletal visitor at the window yesterday did you not Butler?" he asked rubbing his eyes.

Butler looked from the rabbit to the hooman and back again, "The Angel of Death did visit the skeletons' banquet yesterday. But, the Skeleton Guard aren't an army. I mean, they barely do anything right and they wanted nothing to do with the Angel of Death. He isn't doing any harm honest, and he doesn't look like a king."

"Maybe so," said Die knowingly in her best motherly tones, "but he's been killing hoomans Mr Butler. It's still only double figures but we have enough evidence to believe he might be a descendent of the Dawei in scripture and the true king from this prophesy. Butler, don't you think we have good enough reason to go so far as to liaise with the Magician? It's not easy you know. He keeps popping up everywhere," she complained trying to lighten the mood somewhat before turning to the serious matter at hand. "The World Above can't ignore the World Beneath any longer. The hoomans deserve to carry on living and we plan to do anything necessary. Do you understand where I'm going with this?"

"I think she speaks some sense," said Tovey, "and the Children of Light assured me that talking with Topsiders wasn't against Kurbaga's Law. I do have a question though."

The hooman gestured for the rabbit to continue, "Isn't Topside already attacking the World Beneath East?"

"Not yet. It's the kingdom of Normange that's had the worst of the magic explosions based on the papers," said the hooman. "We've actually taken in a lot of refugees from the World Beneath East. We've given them citizenship. They used to be our fellow Topsiders a long time ago so I'm not surprised. I actually have a photo of the Topsider family living with me. They printed one out for me which was very sweet."

The kedi and the rabbit leaned in feeling perplexed and sure enough, in the unmoving photo was a group of hooman like creatures, undeniably World Beneath Easters, standing arm in arm with Die at a pretty Topsider cottage.

The hooman placed the photo back in her purse and pushed the Angel Killer towards Butler, "All I'm asking is for you to pull the trigger if the Angel of Death magics up a skeleton army. He's dangerous so I won't ask you to be reckless. Just keep this with you. If a skeleton army awakens they will kill you and anyone else unfortunate enough to be around. They follow their king to replace the old world with theirs. Make no mistake on that. The Angel of Death seems to be drawn to your hostel so the Federation of Riland has agreed that we need to protect you and the Hostel to Another World. The Twilight World is the neutral in between for all of our worlds after all and we believe that getting rid of Dawei ensures the safety of us all. Think on it and keep this. Our gift to you."

Die placed the gun in Butler's hooman paw and stood up to leave, "Oh and Tovey," said the hooman looking back, "much of the Priest-hood would be very happy for hoomans to be wiped out so best to keep this prophesy as our little secret."

Tovey grimaced, "I can't promise that."

"It'll be your own downfall," she waved back casually.

At that, Dianna Lions-White of the Federation of Riland left the two companions to contemplate their misfortune of falling into a Topsider's plot.

Butler sighed, "I do hope I'll see the Angel of Death again."

"I have to admit Butler," laughed Tovey sitting down next to the fire, relieved at his return to full Magic Rabbit size now that they had returned to the Twilight. "I always thought that if there ever were a fool who could appear before Dawei or any angel without their knees knocking, they're either braver than most or else just plain daft. I be-lieve you're the latter."

"I want to see him," replied Butler. "Besides, there's no way he could magic skeletons from thin air and he really can't be a king. He's more like a pet or a stray puppy since I feed him through the window."

"Think of yourself sometimes would you? Have a sense of mortality! Even the skeletons are terrified of 'their reaper'," barked Tovey exasper-atedly bringing his paw down on the table with a crash, a shudder, and a rumble.

Tovey and Butler paused and frowned. They looked up at the falling dust from the rafters and to one another in alarm.

Crash!

It was even louder this time with a flurry of dust that stung the little kedi's eyes.

"The hooman!" they both shouted at one another in realisation, bolting towards the stairs.

The Angel Killer felt cold. It lay in wait, hidden under Butler's dinner jacket, firmly in paw, loaded and ready for whatever awaited them.

Please don't take Chise away.

The little kedi shook his little fluffy face and turned to his large companion as they came to the grand doors of Butler's homemade function room, "On the count of 3. 1, 2, 3!"

Eight

When Silver Threads Meet

"It won't open!" shouted Butler as he pushed and pushed at the door with all his might.

"Something must be blocking it," replied Tovey. "Stand back!"

The Magic Rabbit took a few hops back and ran at the doors, hitting them very hard indeed and smacking his face in the process. They still did not open. "Ow."

"Don't tell me you're already injured," said Butler in exasperation. "Stop fooling around. Let's take a secret passageway," said the kedi drawing an opening on the wall with a paintbrush.

Tovey grumbled something about making it bigger next time but Butler was already scrambling full speed towards the crashing sounds, soon to be merely whiskers away from who or what was causing them. Tovey really had no choice but to follow. Thank goodness he used to be an avid caver. He wriggled like a worm and pushed himself through to find the utter destruction within.

There was the Angel of Death sitting hunched up only a handful of metres away. Its eyes gleamed cold and glazed as it swayed slightly from side to side. Butler held his breath and crept towards an upturned wardrobe more quietly than a mouse. Tovey tripped upon entry to the dark gloomy room on what was likely one of the fallen lamps. The

Angel of Death growled startled, crawling and sniffing, its eyes shining menacingly through the dark. There was a soft sniffling but Butler could not see where it was coming from. A strange thick quiet settled as all creatures tried to adjust to the darkness engulfing them. A lamp went on from the corner of the room and Butler peeped round to see Chise wiping her eyes with a handkerchief, calmly putting the lamp the right way up so that it could hop onto higher ground. Butler looked over her carefully and happily confirmed that she had made a full recovery and was now a proper hooman size.

The Angel of Death started to hiss and was now on high alert, unhappy to have been interrupted. Butler tried to stop blinking, barely moving as his stiff little body seemed to creek. This was a desperate situation. They needed to get the hooman away, out of this horrible danger. They would have to fight. He could kill the Angel of Death right now with the Angel Killer if he wanted but somehow, that simply did not sit comfortably with him. The monster had not actually tried to kill anyone as far as they knew and it was always alone. In his eyes, the Angel of Death really was more like a lost puppy looking for a place to call home.

I wonder if its lonely?

An understanding with a hint of pity welled up inside Butler's chest as he watched the skeletal winged creature pace the room. The kedi trembled. He knew the madness of loneliness. He signed to Tovey who was standing like a statue, desperately trying not to squeak the floorboard. They spoke in a childish made up sign language for a fleeting moment, agreeing with a nod and breathing in deep, steadying their resolve. Butler grabbed onto his resolve and flung a vase at a nearby wall, running in the opposite direction. Tovey meanwhile bounded over to the hooman, commanding the Children of Light to wait downstairs. The lamp went out dutifully for the companions and blended them into the darkness, hiding them away.

Butler leaped straight over The Angel of Death's head and jumped away from its snarling attack. He jumped so high in fact that he barely missed hitting the battered unhappy rafters. The Angel of Death grabbed at the darkness with its skeletal hand as Butler flashed over him, hissing as its hand cut through thin air.

"Put me down you big brute!" shrieked Chise hitting Tovey with her granny fists as he held her in a fireman's lift.

"Huh? What do you mean? I'm saving you," he protested in surprise.

"I didn't say I needed saving! Put me down! I need to talk to him!" she cried.

A flicker of a silver light appeared at Chise's wrist adding a cool glow to the scene. Tovey put her down before she got the chance to seriously whack him. Chise stepped forwards and her kind eyes glittered as she outstretched her arm to the monster, "Don't you remember me?"

Silver threads burst from the first, pulsing, snaking, winding, unravelling, and intertwining, filling the room with silver veins. They intertwined carefully to create a single thread burning brightest of all, pulsing from hooman to monster. Tovey had wisely burrowed himself into a nearby cupboard whilst Butler stood his ground, unwilling to miss even a second. The Angel of Death looked more civilised now as he followed the silver thread on all fours towards Chise's outstretched hand. His wings scraped and scratched on the floor and those regal eyes looked knowingly at the woman before them.

Just as the Angel of Death had crept up close enough to touch Chise's hand, he stopped and looked up at her lovingly.

"You always come," she smiled taking a step forwards and reaching out, "Dawei."

"Dawei!" shouted the Magic Rabbit popping his head out of the cupboard. "Butler, do it! What are you waiting for?"

Dawei looked over at the little kedi pointing the Angel Killer from the corner and narrowed his eyes. With a glance upwards, he shot out his skeletal wing, sending Butler flying into a pile of beanbags.

The ceiling suddenly decided that this was enough excitement for one day and with a great old creak started collapsing, missing Butler's toes by an inch.

"Butler! Butler!" shouted Tovey bouncing out of his hiding place, coughing through the dust. He pushed through the hanging planks and bits of broken wood. "Oh thank Kurbaga. Are you quite alright you daft cat?"

Butler pushed himself to his feet feeling thoroughly winded but not broken, "Are you done hiding Mr Priestly Rabbit? What of the hooman?"

The kedi and the Magic Rabbit watched a dusty Dawei open up his wings to reveal a beaming Chise who had not even a scratch to show for all the rubble Butler would soon need to clean. The companions let out a huge sigh of relief. Having a hooman die on site would be awfully bad for the hostel's ratings. The silver thread was shining from wrist to wrist, connecting the two souls through time, joining their two worlds together for a moment, however fleeting.

Chise placed her hooman paw on the side of Dawei's cheek, brushing his white hair from his eyes, being careful not to disturb the mask. "Time never did run smoothly for us," she whispered warmly.

There was a clink of metal. Dawei startled and looked up to see the Magic Rabbit picking up the Angel Killer. With a click of his fingers, Dawei disappeared and reappeared in the window that opened obligingly for him. With one last look at his hooman, he took off into the crimson sky, gliding swiftly away from it all. The old woman ran to the window like a child and watched the Angel of Death disappear into the clouds.

"Farewell old friend," she whispered.

The forever morning sun carried her tears upwards as she hugged her hooman paws to her chest, "Could you leave me alone for a while?" she asked softly.

Tovey put a great big paw on Butler's shoulder and turned him towards the doors, "Let's go. Help me move that wardrobe."

Indeed that seemed to be the culprit for the locked double doors and Butler helped move the wardrobe by supervising and dictating where it needed to be placed. With one last glance back, Butler followed the Magic Rabbit out, leaving the hooman at the window.

"You sure it's okay to leave her?" asked the kedi.

Tovey looked him in the eyes and replied softly, "I think it was the only caring thing we could do."

Butler nodded and a hint of guilt crept in, "Do you think she will be mad at us for trying to kill her boyfriend?"

"Boyfriend?" Tovey spat laughing heartily. "Oh Kurbaga have mercy on us. That's the last thing we need!"

"I'm serious!" Butler moaned.

With a hearty slap on the back to which Butler almost tripped over, Tovey grinned and suggested they make a fancy lunch. "Food always makes me feel better!"

After racing upstairs and changing their attire, the two companions went to work their magic in the kitchen to the delight of the ferrets who all appeared claiming to have finished their morning rounds. After some grumbling from Tovey they were all handed out kitchen jobs and a mini feast was prepared in record time.

"That should just about do it," beamed Tovey happily thinking of nothing but food.

Butler gave the thumbs up and the ferrets scurried out carrying all manners of plates, saucers, bowls, and buckets of Butler's special harvester curry. He was very domesticated you see so making a large lunch for a hoard of ferrets was actually an easy endeavour for him. Butler however, was not thinking about the food at all and had done his part quietly on autopilot. He had in fact been thinking about many things, speaking only when spoken to, and frowning an awful lot. The little kedi trudged out and placed the utensils in front of the excited hungry ferrets sighing, comforted by their happy little faces.

"Hello Butler," came a kind voice.

Butler looked up and sure enough, the hooman was sat next to the fire, leaning in as if she had been interrupted in the midst of a deep conversation.

What do you want?

Butler had been thinking very hard on what the angel had said and he was starting to have an idea of what would lead him to his answer.

"Hello Miss Hooman," he said happily walking over to her.

She didn't look mad at him at all. She was as warm and welcoming as she had always been, a bit like what Butler imagined a family would feel like.

What do I want?

The first part of his answer was helpfully sitting right in front of him. The second, well, the kedi had a feeling he knew where to find that one as well.

Butler savoured the thought for a moment before plucking up the courage to let the words travel through the air, "I'll be going on an adventure, if you'd care to join me," he said bowing slightly.

There was a quiet between them, interrupted only by the buzzing of the happy eaters behind them and the whispers of the Children of Light from the fire. Looking up, Butler's determined gaze met the kind shiny eyes of a hooman for the first time. He offered out his paw to welcome her, "Miss Chise."

Nine

A Trial by Fire

"Splendid, count me in!" said the golden ferret enthusiastically.

"Why are you here?" asked the startled Butler. "Never mind. Yes, you can come too."

We'll do well with the Magician's protection. Who knows what might be waiting for us down there. Chise glanced over at the Children of Light who gave a hearty thumbs up and a why not?

She looked up to the kedi, "I think I'd like that Mr Butler. I've always wanted to see what was in that vault of yours."

How did she know we were going to the vault?

The ferret hopped in excitement, "You cheeky devil. I bet you have all manners of riches hoarded in there. Can I steal something?"

The Butler patted the ferret's head teasingly, "We will be retrieving something, something important. It's actually been calling out to me for some time now but I've been ignoring it," he said shyly, "but I'm afraid there aren't quite the riches you're hoping for. Tovey are you coming?" Tovey had a mouth full of food of course and gestured for a repeat. "Would you like to come on an adventure with us after lunch?"

Tovey thoughtfully chewed and swallowed, "I'll stay here and see if I can convince the Children of Light to work with me in creating a stronger defence for the hostel. I hope by the name of Kurbaga that it won't be needed but it's been a long time since I did the last magical maintenance."

Butler agreed heartily with the idea and ushered all present to set themselves down for lunch. It's no good going on an adventure on an empty stomach after all.

With bellies full, the kedi, the Magician, and the hooman took the paternoster lift embodied with magic for convenience. They got off clumsily at the lowest point, as the Magician took his hooman-like form to perform some simple safety checks. The tunnel looked like the inside of a cave and was winding on and on.

"Okay Boss!" said Cian cheerfully retrieving his magic back in a single swoosh.

As they went forwards the glow grew and grew, and a steady repeating rumbling echoed louder and louder.

As the hooman clung to the sleeve of the kedi for balance she tugged on it and asked the question, "Do you have a pet, Butler? A big one perhaps?"

"It really does sound ginormous," chimed the Magician, brushing his perfect blond locks from his forehead. "Was it expensive? Is it rare?"

"I don't own any pets," replied Butler with dread. "Not to my knowledge that is."

It had been far too long since he'd checked up on things and he feared for the worst. The rumbling was now very clearly the sounds of a very large creature snoring in its sleep.

"Oh excellent! I'm looking forward to this!" sang Cian skipping ahead.

They turned another corner and came across what looked to be a giant safety cabinet with a locked drawer at the top.

The kedi was just about to trot over to the long ladder when Cian clapped his palms together, "Let's take the shortcut shall we? Hold on tight Miss Hooman," he added, turning to Chise and taking her free hooman paw before Butler could voice any opinion on the matter. "Up we go!"

Up up up they went, gracefully hovering at the drawer's lock. It really was handy having a magician around. Butler unclipped a small key from his tucked away necklace and with a click the drawer welcomed them in. They whizzed all the way down what would have been a five minute ladder climb in mere seconds.

"There we go," said the Magician hovering them inches off the floor gracefully. "Now, if you'll excuse me."

With a squeak, Cian transformed into a golden ferret and started trotting off.

"Where are you going?" Butler called out startled by this sudden change.

"To watch," squeaked the ferret speedily climbing up to a high perch and magicking his favourite Lady Grey tea. A second ferret appeared from an impromptu transparent chute and gladly accepted a small ceramic teacup.

"Is that Dotty?" Butler asked out loud trying to peer up. "Lazy Magician," he huffed.

"It must be very carefree having the profession of magician," helpfully chimed Chise.

"How nice for him," Butler grumbled.

The golden ferret stood up on its hind legs and called down to them, "Look at the fish of the air. They do not buy or sell or store away in vaults, and yet the mighty Kurbaga feeds them. Are you not much more valuable than they?"

Butler put his paws to his mouth, "Cast but a glance at riches, and they are gone, for they will surely sprout wings and fly off to the sky like a dragon," he called back before then adding more for his own benefit, "I know. I know in my head. I just need to teach it to my heart."

He did like having things. He did like money. He always looked to make more and enjoyed sending it to his secret vault. It never seemed to be enough. If only his heart could stop.

There was a tentative tug on his sleeve and Butler looked down to see the hooman mouth a single word, "Dragon."

It was true. A golden dragon lay, with great big wings folded and feet carefully tucked. Behind it there were all manners of Butler's precious things laying in disorder: moving photos, a kedi sized plane, a number of childhood teddy bears, and a small sword collection amongst other clutter. However, one could be forgiven for not noticing those things with a great big dragon in the way. The golden creature slept peacefully on what looked like a bed of coins that it had likely hoarded from the tips jar. To say that Butler was surprised would be an unfair appraisal. He stood there with gaping jaw. After all, there really are no words to express an unwelcome pet dragon.

"You've come at last," said Butler's voice from behind a pile of old newspapers.

That was strange. Butler closed his mouth. A figure stepped out and began walking towards them. "I've been waiting so very long. How filthy of you to bring a hooman to our home."

Butler's jaw opened wide once more. It really was him.

"Who's that?" Chise asked seeing very well that Butler was just as dumbfounded and could not help answer this question.

The Butler figure stopped a few metres away and bowed slightly, "My apologies, how rude of me. I am a piece of Butler. A fragment of his soul that he misplaced when he left her here all those years ago," he said pointing at the snoozing dragon. "I almost disappeared but I cleverly attached myself to the Gate Key that the Master entrusted to us. Thank goodness I found it too. As if anything less important would have been enough to hold such a soul piece as I."

"Plot twist!" came a shout from up high.

The golden ferret was thoroughly enjoying himself nibbling on a cupcake and certainly had one of the best seats in the house. Butler tried to motion for the Magician to come down and help but quickly found it to be a futile venture.

"Well it was handy of him to tell us so clearly," said Chise trying to lighten the mood. "What are you doing going and misplacing a piece of your soul?" she asked slapping him on the arm. "I presume this isn't what we came for."

Butler rubbed the back of his neck connecting the dots, "Now that

I think about it, I did feel like a piece was missing," he said sheepishly. "An extra piece that is. Oopsie."

Chise whacked his arm again with more power than a granny should have, "Don't you oopsie me. Where is that Gate Key? It sounds important. I'll go fetch it for us."

Where is the Gate Key? Butler had no idea where he had put it. It had been years since he'd been down here last. *Butler you fool!* His blank expression said it all.

"Now that's settled," said the soul piece theatrically clicking his little boots together. "Precious, won't you wake up and play?"

The golden dragon opened its eyes in an instant and reared its great big head high, smiling to show an impressive double set of razor sharp teeth. With no hesitation she flew up and raced through the cavern, licking the cave sides with flame, beating her great wings with a noise like thunder. Flickering fires danced up and down the walls as the precious items nearest to them turned to soot. It was almost like the dragon was putting on a show for its visitors.

"It's time to die dear Butler," said the soul piece menacingly. "I'm sure I would be a better fit for that weak body of ours. Imagine all the adventures I could have if I had our body!"

Butler stiffened at this strangely evil Butler. *What a predicament.*

"Chise," he whispered, "please find the Gate Key. I'm so terribly sorry. I don't know where it is, but it's a small brass key with an engraving of crossbones on it. I'll distract the evil me and the pet dragon I didn't know I had."

She didn't need asking twice. Chise saluted and hopped off to it, careful to go in between the most precious objects that she hoped the dragon would not want to loose.

"Now then," muttered the little kedi, "evil me is probably as weak as I am, but what do I do about my angry pet dragon?"

The beast stood tall, growling and ready to hunt.

The Magic Rabbit meanwhile, was diligently working with the

Children of Light to strengthen the hostel with magic should it ever come under an unfair attack.

This included many arguments of course and Tovey found himself unwittingly raising his voice more than once, "Would you stop talking? Stop muttering during every instruction I give you. There is absolutely no way you got all of that. You there, what did I just say?"

The little innocently clueless flicker of flame stayed silent. "See?" shouted the rabbit waving his paws. "Right, once more from the top. This is the last time I'm saying this."

This of course was a lie. Tovey sat and drilled the fire through five more times before finally flopping down onto the comfy sofa in victory and defeat. This was a short lived luxury.

"You're being summoned Mr Teacher Rabbit. Off you go, shoo shoo," piped up the fire happily. "Get ready for your trip!" they chirped to the clueless rabbit slowly snapping back to the world.

"Huh? What are you..."

The sofa opened up beneath him, letting his bottom float for a strange moment before plummeting him down into the depths of who knows where. The Children of Light didn't once consider how in the world he was going to get out again of course or what was awaiting him at the other end.

"Master's orders," they shouted down, closing the makeshift laundry chute so that there could be no climbing back up.

"I'm a priest! How dare youahhhhh!" shouted the rabbit indignantly as his world went black.

The chute went straight on like a tunnel for some way like a very deep well. Either the tunnel was very deep, or Tovey was falling very slowly, for he had plenty of time to think and look around grumpily with crossed arms. At first, he tried to look around and down to get a clue as to where he was coming to, but it was far too dark to see anything at all but the fleeting shadows who looked equally lost.

"Well this is inconvenient," said Tovey to himself as his two stomachs jiggled uncomfortably. "After falling this much I suppose I'll be able to fall off just about anything without batting an eye. That is, if those idiot flames don't forget to save me from broken bones at the bottom."

It was as if he had spoken the magic words. The rabbit found himself slowing to an impressive thud. He was stuck. Tovey felt relieved to have stopped and yet his back paws seemed to have entered a very hot room.

It felt a little concerning that he was dangling bottom first in a mystery destination, "A little help," he called up to the nothingness.

With the echoes of faint laughter the opening widened and Tovey fell into a burning red room. In fact, that was real fire engulfing a kite in front of his twitching nose. The Magic Rabbit hopped up in surprise and looked around, coming face to face with a giant golden dragon. His heart jumped into his two stomachs as he gulped in horror.

"I've been waiting for you Mr Fancy Rabbit," said the beast in a voice as sweet as pie.

"Oh hell no!" cried Tovey as he darted to his safe tunnel but of course found nothing but a solid wall.

The horrible sounds of the dragon's laughter echoed in the stony hollows far above and its hot breath made the poor rabbit's eyes water.

I can't even hide. Well, it might have been easier to get past a dragon if I were a ferret. I'd be smaller, much less easy to see from such a frightful way up. Was that the hooman messing around opening drawers? Why is it always me?

The Magic Rabbit resorted to the only thing he could do, run! The game of tag had begun. The dragon delightedly followed the rabbit as he hop hop hopped in and out of sight, sparking up conversation as if catching up with an old friend, "How marvellous of you to drop by my dear rabbit after you left me for so long! Did you come because you needed something? Perhaps you came for my money? Or perhaps you got kicked out of your fancy Priesthood?"

Tovey was equally confused dear reader but he was not quite so unlearned in dragons as to deny such a claim, "No thank you, most beautiful dragon," he called back. "I did not come to beg or to ask for what is yours. I only wanted to see you and see for myself how perfect you are. They said that nothing as perfect as a dragon could exist out of children's books but I, I did not believe them."

"Did you now?" mused the dragon blushing slightly.

Tovey thought he saw Butler, or more than one Butler for the fleeting of a second before he took a sharp turn to avoid a flicker of fire from the dragon's open jaw. He had to keep it talking.

"No fairytales or picture books could prepare your innocent servant for such a spectacular reality. You have beautiful eyes " yelled the Magic Rabbit panting.

"You're being very nice to me aren't you, you little heartbreaker?" asked the dragon rhetorically. "It seems you might have forgotten me."

Then the dragon really did laugh. It was an ear piercing, booming sound that shook the cavern walls.

Tovey was flummoxed, "Who are you?"

"Who am I?" snorted the dragon spouting a sea of fire that licked at the rabbit's paw tips.

It was an unfortunately badly timed question. Tovey gasped as the dragon shot flame after flame to catch him as he hopped round giant wardrobes and dressers.

"Learn to read the situation, Tovey you idiot!" he shouted into the air.

It became a favourite life lesson of his for years to come, passing it on to all who were as unfortunately clueless as he. *Think you stupid rabbit. You've not done your time in this adventure just yet.*

The kedi watched as the Magic Rabbit came dropping in, stealing the dragon's full attention, and even helpfully running in the opposite direction having what looked like a pleasant conversation. Butler was also keeping an eye on Chise, who was currently precariously climbing up giant dressing tables like a spider with magic gloves on both hands and feet. *Must be the Magician's doing.* The Magician of course, was now serving high tea with a second batch of Lady Grey to Dotty who Butler was starting to have his suspicions about. Only those with secrets make friends with magicians.

"Now then, what to do with this evil me?" he muttered under his breath, turning to the task at hand.

The soul piece had already tried slapping Butler to no avail and now had resorted to throwing objects in his general direction. One thing had lead to another and now Butler found himself swinging off a chandelier no less. It was a very silly battle. The most ridiculous in all of Butler's experiences to come. Incidentally, this may in fact have been the reason that the story was fondly recounted long afterwards. None of them really did anything heroic in it. In fact, none of them were really in any form of danger at all. No one other than perhaps Tovey, who was now trying to use magical origami to blind a fire breathing dragon leading to even more fire breathing. The chandelier wasn't exactly helping Butler avoid all the little objects flying his way from the frustrated soul piece. It did however help in getting out of the way, especially from all that dragon drama.

"I wish it had been me."

There were no flying objects. Butler looked down and to his surprise, the soul piece was looking rather down. "I wish he'd chosen me!" he shouted clutching his chest.

At this, Butler found himself floating with some sort of magic. Chise, also floating, was now swimming through the air towards him brandishing a small brass key with crossbones, "I found it," she said gleefully.

"No wait! Please don't make me go back! Please!" cried the soul piece. "Not yet," it sobbed, "please."

This was of course more than enough to pull at the hooman's motherly heartstrings, "It's never easy to leave is it Butler?" she asked the soul piece who startled at the surprise of hearing that name used for the likes of him. "Why don't we all join the Magician and his apprentice for a spot of tea whilst Tovey kindly entertains the angry dragon? In fact, there's something I'd like to tell you. Both of you."

Ten

A Holy Intervention

The walls began to expand and shrink as giant bubbles drifted here and there. The hooman nodded and the Magician poured tea into little teacups that seemed to simply pop out of his sleeve as commanded. They shared a knowing glance and bid everyone feel comfortable up on that ledge at the highest point of the cavern. Even the dragon came over with Tovey hanging by the scruff, plopping him down to gratefully accept a teacup and a biscuit. And when each creature and hooman and all in between had got their cup of tea, each fell into a peaceful quiet with a sigh of contentment. The bubbles floated and glided, multiplying silently, filling the room, careful not to touch the companions or risk being noticed. Not yet at least.

"And now," said the Magician, watching the bubbles from the corner of his eye, careful not to draw attention to what was coming, "if you please Miss Chise."

Chise looked out over the floating orbs and cleared her throat, "Thank you my dear. And welcome Miss Dragon and Mr Tovey, do help yourself to more biscuits," she said smiling, passing the bowl over for Tovey to offer to the giant monster nudging him. "Now then, Mr Butler," she said addressing the soul piece, "may I ask you how you feel about being the soul piece and not currently having the kedi body?"

The soul piece flushed crimson and looked down at his teacup before bravely looking the hooman in the eye, "I'm the evil one. I'm the evil part of Butler. That's why Master took me out and left me here when Butler wasn't paying attention. I wasn't chosen to have the kedi body," he announced matter-of-factly before welling up slightly, "but I wish it had been me," he added in a whisper.

Chise placed her hooman paw on his tiny little shoulder and gave it a reassuring squeeze, "Thank you so much for your bravery and honesty Mr Butler. You could do with being less mysterious Mr Cian," she added teasingly.

The Magician looked away uncharacteristically, "Mysterious suits me just fine."

Butler felt rather badly for the soul piece. If he'd known he'd been left down here he would have at least come to play with him from time to time. Maybe they could have ridden the kedi plane together.

"But you know Mr Butler," Chise continued as she leant in towards the soul piece, "there will come a time when Butler cannot continue and will need you to take the baton in this little thing called life. I think you were given life as a soul piece for a reason," she said knowingly. "Your time may not have come, but mark my words, it will come. And as we work towards that time when we can shine, let us clap for those whose time has come now. I believe life happens for us, not to us. Your time will come."

She leant back and lifted her teacup to the soul piece with a great warm smile.

The soul piece shuffled and fiddled with his paws, "Do you really believe I'll get to live in the future too Miss Hooman?"

"Everything's possible in our worlds of magic. Your master isn't as evil as you both may believe. When you leap through time as he does you do become clumsy with the way you do things, always in a rush as you can imagine," she said happily recalling all of the things she knew that he should have said. *Silly man.* "But in all the things he didn't say, was there ever a doubt that he loved you? Both of you?"

The two little kedis looked shyly at one another.

"And what does his love mean? Does it mean he's forgotten you because he's not physically here right now? Does it mean he doesn't see you in his future plans? Does being a soul piece right now mean you're any less loved?" asked Chise.

The soul piece shook his little head. He could feel his time outside the key running to its end. He leant in and hugged Butler, "Make sure you don't forget about me. I'm here to take the baton when you find you can run no more. But make sure you run a good race for us now," he smiled and looked from the hooman, back to the body he once had, "I'll be waiting."

A floating rainbow bubble touched the soul piece, bursting silently. Butler squeaked in surprise as Tovey coughed on a piece of biscuit. The soul piece had fallen soundly asleep in an instant for seemingly no reason, peacefully dreaming of his better life. Chise placed the small brass key into Butler's paw. He nodded stiffly and touched the key to the sleeping kedi, storing him away for a future time, for another world, and a better life. Butler gripped the key tightly in his fluffy paw, making a silent vow for the future and the kedi he would become.

"Who's next? Is it me, is it me?" piped up the dragon grinning, a terrifying sight indeed.

This outburst shook the little kedi back and he breathed, counting from three, before standing up and humbly bowing to the beast, "I'm sorry," he said pausing. "I'm sorry I left you here. I'm sorry I didn't come and visit like I promised. I'm sorry we got separated. I wanted to find some news, any hint on how to reverse it all, so that I could come tell you. But, but I'm sorry my heart, I found nothing!" he said with aching chest bowing further still. "I found nothing."

"Your heart?" came a chorus of astonishment.

Tovey pointed and stuttered, "Your heart is a d-dragon?"

The process in which his heart had learnt to become a dragon was a mystery to the kedi also but there was no denying it, the beast that towered the cavern was the very same heart he had locked away all those years ago.

The dragon purred and its eyes flashed their brilliant pink as it looked upon the body it once gave life to, "We could have looked together. Did you hate me? Is that why you locked me in here?" asked the dragon breathing a heavy sigh, waving its paw at the cavern around them.

To this, the little kedi stood up tall and looked the beast bravely in the eyes, "I don't hate you. I could never hate you. What a silly conclusion," he said feeling frustrated already. "It's because you're needy! You never shut up even when I try to physically restrain you. You always tell the truth and that's not fair!" he huffed and stomped with his little kedi foot.

All those painfully embarrassing exchanges and ruined acquaintances. "Haven't you heard of the phrase of holding your heart on your sleeve? Well it's not fun for me! I don't want to be that!"

The dragon thought long and hard on this. It had many fond memories of teasing the little kedi but now it could remember being scolded just as often, "My name shall be Silence because I must stay silent," it concluded.

"What? No, that's a silly name," Butler started to protest, "that's..."

"No more silly than Butler or Cian the Magician," the dragon taunted before swiftly clamping its own mouth with giant deadly paws, realising the truth telling habit was indeed one to be worked on. "Wasn't me."

Cian thoroughly enjoyed that one and rolled around with laughter almost knocking his teacup, "Good one! Can we keep it? Please?" he begged.

The dragon did a wriggle at this and made the cutest face it could muster, which wasn't particularly cute at all, but they could all see that the beast was trying.

"That's why we're here," replied Butler with a smile holding out his paw to the dragon. "Will you please help me be more honest Silence. Let's find a way to live again, together."

The dragon reared its menacing face in delight and in a poof of smoke, a girl with startlingly pink hair and golden yellow eyes leaped towards Butler from the air. On her way down, a floating rainbow bubble popped and Butler's heart became a tiny golden dragon, peacefully asleep as it continued to fall. Thank goodness for it too, or else our poor Butler would have not been able to so gracefully catch her. The little dragon was stowed safely into the kedi's shirt breast pocket where she began to snore quietly, occasionally kicking Butler as she fought his enemies in her dreams.

The Magician cheerfully poured out some more tea and looked around the circle, "I wonder who's next. I wonder if it's you Miss Chise," he said turning to the hooman representative of the group.

She giggled, "Oh don't mind me," replied the hooman. "I'm just on one last vacation. This story isn't about me. It's the beginning of his."

The kedi didn't hear this part as he had suddenly been engulfed by a giant Magic Rabbit. Tovey never did explain this sudden display of affection and Silence was knocked out for the count so couldn't weigh in either. However, there is a lot that can be said without words and in this moment, it's possible that no words would have been enough.

"Here, take this," said Butler handing over the Gate Key.

Tovey let him out of the bear hug and gaped, "That's your soul piece man. Are you mad? I can't take that!" he said panicked.

Having the responsibility of not loosing a piece of someone's soul and keeping the key that opens the gates of the worlds safe was indeed a big responsibility.

Butler pushed it into Tovey's paw, "Please take it. There's no good in me keeping it locked away waiting for thieves," Butler said using his best begging eyes. "Please. You're the only one I can trust with it."

"Rude," interjected the Magician.

"I wouldn't trust you with a bus ticket, let alone a Gate Key," laughed Chise. "You'd probably forget what it was and lose it in a magical rift in your floorboards. You really should fix those properly you know so that they stop crawling back."

Cian couldn't argue with that one and stuck his tongue out play-fully, admitting his defeat. The Magic Rabbit reluctantly took one of the most important items of the worlds and stowed it into the deepest layer of his magical pouch, next to his boat and his crossbow. "Don't tell anyone I have it," he said nervously looking at all present.

They nodded vigorously and vowed that it was safest to forget its existence entirely for the time being.

All of a sudden, Tovey's eyes glistened and a funny look appeared on his fluffy face. It was time for Mr Tovey the Magic Rabbit to be on duty. With crumbs still on his whiskers, Tovey opened his mouth and his best priestly voice boomed out with authority:

"I saw seven golden lamp stands hopping on silver gloves. Among the lamp stands was someone like a hooman son, dressed in a robe reaching down to his feet and with a golden sash around his chest. The hair on his head was like silk, as white as snow, and his eyes were like blazing fire. His feet were like bronze glowing in a furnace filled with the Children of Light, and his voice was like the sound of rushing living waters. In his right hand he held seven stars, and coming out of his mouth was a sharp, double-edged sword of justice. His face was like the sun of Twilight, shining the magic hour in all its brilliance.

When I saw him, I fell at his feet as though death had found me.

Then he placed his skeletal hand on me and said, 'Do not be afraid. I am the First and the Last. I am the Origin. I was dead, and now look, I am alive for ever and ever! I hold the keys of life and death so that all those who seek, shall find their eternal life in me.'

A bubble popped on Tovey's ear and he began to snooze in a seated position, unusually perfectly balanced. At this, a very different voice took over and at Tovey's shoulder, floating in a golden orb, appeared a froglike creature with many arms and many legs. This frog of course, was the creator of the worlds - Kurbaga the Master of Creation.

"Go," he commanded to the Magician, Chise, and Dotty the ferret who had been somewhat forgotten but had been very happy to simply eat biscuits in great company.

"Yes Master," replied Cian in a serious tone.

Throwing the ferret and the hooman into his teapot, the Magician dutifully bowed low, disappearing in an instant.

Butler fell to his knees like a good little kedi and peered up as the Master spoke:

"I have heard your prayers. I know your struggles and your chains, so why are you still sleeping? Wake up and walk boldly forwards to reclaim the life that is rightfully yours! I know your deeds. You have a reputation of being alive, busying yourself to forget what you lost. You look alive but you are dead. Wake up! Strengthen what remains and is about to die, for I have found your deeds unfinished.

Hold this close to heart, and leave the past behind you for your new life. But if you do not wake up, if you do not break your chains, I will come collect you like a thief, and you will not know at what time I will come for you.

These are my words to the worlds, the words of the Amen, the faithful and true witness, the ruler of creation:

I know you, that you are neither cold nor hot. I wish you were either one or the other! So, because you are lukewarm, living halfheartedly even with the blessings of magic, I have started the catalyst that will shake the worlds to awaken from their boring slumber.

I know about the mischief of those who say they are the Priesthood and are not, weaving the church for self-satisfaction. To those who have ears, let you hear what the Children of Light say to you. My church has no walls and my Children of Light will always find you. The one who walks my path and is victorious will not be hurt at all by the second death."

At this, the Master of Creation rose in his golden orb, calling the bubbles up to the highest point of the cavern with great swirling winds. Butler clutched his jacket and placed a gentle paw on the sleeping dragon. The kedi squinted as multicoloured rain fell silently all around him. With a hop, he began smiling wide as he watched the droplets wash over the fire and soot that his daft heart had left behind. With the swirling winds carrying them, the pretty rainbow drops explored and evaporated, leaving his cavern sparkling clean.

The kedi gave the Master a little clap. Kurbaga chuckled and sighed, drawing in close, speaking softly, "Do not be afraid of what you are about to suffer Butler. The church will turn against you. The worlds will turn against you. I tell you, Iskelet Kral will put your friends in prison to test them, and many will suffer persecution. Be faithful, even to the point of death, and I will give you life without chains as your victor's crown.

The time will come for you Mr Butler to choose. Will you walk along the path to break the chains of the very World Beneath that betrayed you?"

Kurbaga handed Butler the map of the worlds that Tovey had picked up earlier and neglected to mention, "I daresay you know what I want you to do with this," he said placing the little magical scroll into Butler's paw. "She will lead you to your slumbering Skeleton King," he said calmly, showing a flicker of an image. "She's not exactly a good hooman but I will use her for many of the necessary breakthroughs to come. It's not a nice job Butler but I trust you to get it done. Be faithful, even to the point of death, and I will give you your life without chains," repeated the Master of Creation.

Butler tucked the scroll into a large handy inner jacket pocket without answering. What does one say to the Master of everything when he tells you to betray what should have been his favourite world? There really was no place to hide from the Master of the worlds. *The catalyst to wake up the worlds? It has felt like things have been a touch too lively lately.*

"If I refuse?" asked the little kedi out of curiosity.

"Your chains will be all you ever know for eternity," replied Kurbaga ominously.

"If I betray the World Beneath, I can break my chains and live?" asked Butler to confirm the arrangement.

Kurbaga chuckled, "Youth always was hasty. You will be my catalyst and from that catalyst you will find your breaker of chains. Wake up and live Mr Butler, slave of the Hostel to Another World!"

Eleven

Goodbye Old Friends

There stood Butler, blinking back the tears that blinded him. As he lay the slowly awakening Tovey down to snooze in an armchair next to the fire, the kedi looked from the forlorn Cian down to Chise lying on the floor. Through his hastily brushed away tears he could see that she lay motionless and pale.

"But I've only been gone for an hour," he said uncomprehending, disbelieving.

Butler carefully knelt next to her and her eyes opened as if she had been waiting for him.

She smiled as Butler took her hooman paw into his, "Hello Butler of the Hostel to Another World," she whispered warmly. "As you can see, my time has run out. It's time for me to say goodbye and to join those who left before me."

The hooman brushed the teardrop from the little kedi's cheek. "Don't be sad. I've lived a long life. I have no regrets. I saw my closest friends one last time and was even spoilt with one last adventure," she said smiling weakly. "I am glad I lived to this day, that I can go surrounded by my old dear friends, looking out at these golden clouds that I love so very very much."

Butler wanted to speak but could not and busied himself with wiping at his streaming face with his sleeve. "Forgive me," he said at last. "If I had known, I would have done more, been with you more. Please don't go Miss Chise."

The old woman smiled, "It's okay. You did plenty my dear. I even saw him one last time," she said with eyes gazing at things unseen. "Now, you go live a good life Butler. You have a big long life ahead of you. You may not know me, not yet, but I know you. You shall find your answers Butler, my brave brave little kedi."

She looked over to Cian and then gently nodded to the Children of Light. "I'm ready now."

With gladness in her heart, Chise closed her eyes. The Children of Light watched over Chise lovingly as she took her last breath and Butler still unbelieving, stayed crouched by her side, holding his shirt pocket as it snored. The fireplace took on an unusual pink glow as the Children of Light slowly intertwined and expanded outwards, weaving themselves to rest gently beneath her. The pink embers licked at the kedi's whiskers and Butler felt a rush of life flash before his eyes. He knew her. He stood as the truth sunk in.

As the Children of Light made their preparations, the Magician and the kedi stood together silently, barely noticing as Tovey joined them, giving a prayer of safe passage.

"Chise," Butler cried at last. "Chise, why now? Why must it be now? We have magic. Surely there's a magic to bring her back?" he asked turning from magician to rabbit in desperate hope.

They shook their heads.

"I'm sorry Butler," said Tovey. "There are some things that magic cannot do."

He hugged the little kedi tight, uncharacteristically sniffling loudly himself.

"Time never did run smoothly," said the Magician looking beyond the window with a distant look in his eyes.

Without waiting for a response, Cian glided out of the window, hovering slightly to look back at his friend one last time, before plummeting out of sight. He cried secretly as he glided through the clouds, crying louder and louder, screaming as droplets of water hit his face from all sides. His clear voice could be heard calling her name over and over again until that voice became rasp and died out, drowned by the four winds that carried him.

Butler stood there, still blinking through his tears. Tovey sat silently in prayer. Neither spoke. As thoughts slowly formed and then muddled in his mind, Butler brushed away his tears and stooped down to pick up a log to feed the embers. He handed it over to the Children of Light gently, watching them as they worked. Slowly, he sat down again, wondering what one was meant to do in such a situation. He looked out at the crimson clouds marked with grey as a great rain formed beneath the Twilight. It was as if the very skies cried for Chise, for the hooman friend of creatures and magicians, who smiled and welcomed them all. It was through that grey swirling mist above the furthermost clouds that the kedi started to see specs of something coming towards them. *Curious. Perhaps the Magician forgot something.*

The Children of Light raised Chise's body, securing a blanket of cold embers beneath her as they lifted her out towards the sky. Butler watched the flames stretch out towards the door that obligingly swung open for them.

Uncomprehending, he rushed to the doorway and cried, "Where are you taking her? Don't take her from me! Why?"

"It's calling for her," answered Tovey as he came to stand by the kedi's side. He pointed at the now rather large spec walking on the clouds towards them. "All life must end. We must not intervene. She must seek her eternal place on the threshold of the afterlife. It's come to take her there."

They watched side by side as the Children of Light lifted Chise up on a long arm of flickering flames. The sounds of strange bells rang with each footstep as the giant approached. Its body was covered in strange patterns and ancient writings that appeared and faded as they glistened in the sun's rays. The giant flickered, semi-transparent as it dragged its long heavy arms with each laboured step.

Butler looked to his friend as the giant creature began to wail an ancient song, carried by the winds that swirled around it. "It's called an Orakci. It's a harvester of souls," said Tovey putting his great big fluffy paw on Butler's tiny shoulder. "Chise decided to lay to rest in the arms of the Twilight."

They watched the giant lean in towards her, "She chose her mortality, her time to leave the worlds, so that she might save him."

Butler frowned and looked at his friend and saw that his eyes had glazed over once more. Looking back out over the sky, Butler watched nervously as the Orakci sung its last notes and swallowed the hooman's body whole.

The kedi stood there frozen as the Magic Rabbit continued, "Together they will pass to the afterlife, beyond the confines of mortality and the heartaches of our worlds. Her spirit will now pass peacefully on after a life well lived."

So it was that the hooman named Chise was taken back by the worlds, leaving behind the creatures she loved above all else. But although one hooman's time had come to an end, time never did run smoothly.

Butler felt a firm pinch on his shoulder, "We have a problem."

Twelve

A Skeleton Army

The kedi and the Magic Rabbit stood transfixed in horror as they watched the mustering of a skeleton army. The bones crawled towards them on all fours as countless others still clawed their way out of the clouds. This is how a skeleton army descended upon the Twilight, with numbers worthy for a war of kings. Or so it appeared to the two solitary creatures who were shutting the hostel door in haste, though this was actually a rather small skeleton army compared to the full power of a Skeleton King.

"By Kurbaga, what happened to you?" shrieked the rabbit suddenly jumping back.

There stood Butler the kedi, fully grown, as if a decade had passed them by. He was not quite as tall as the Magic Rabbit but with such a strong aura one could be forgiven for unwittingly seeing them as standing on equal measure. Tovey looked him over in bewilderment.

Butler gave himself a quick glance in the window's reflection and then looked back to the rabbit unflustered, "Show me the hostel's new features Mr Priestly Rabbit. We haven't a moment to lose."

They set to work as hard as they could alongside the frantically busy Children of Light who were now racing through the hostel trialling their new custom-made veins of magic. Had Tovey not been carried single-handedly by the kedi no more than an hour ago, he may have not believed the strength he was now witnessing from this slender creature. Butler and Tovey dashed about, filling the hostel with magical incantations and undoing all safety measures that had been holding back the magic within. The little golden dragon pretended to still be asleep and curled up shivering slightly within Butler's breast pocket. Put mildly, this was not magic she approved of.

At last the preparations were complete and a temporary barrier pushed out across the clouds to steer any unwelcome guests elsewhere.

"Right," said Butler, "how bad is it out there?"

The now not so little kedi tried to peer through the largest window and squinted, tilting one way and then the other.

"Use this if you like," said Tovey gruffly, brandishing a pirate's telescope that he'd pulled out from his magic pouch.

"Perfect," replied Butler snatching it up eagerly, putting a fleeting smile on the rabbit's face.

Out across the clouds, there were fountains of skeletal bats that flew erratically, darkening the Twilight's amber glow. Pillars of bones had climbed the Orakci that sluggishly brushed them off in big felling swoops. The natural process in which the hooman had been taken had seemingly displeased Dawei who was screaming up high above it all. His screams turned into skeletal eagles, wolves, porcupines and from the confused clouds falling upwards rushed golden rain, painting the ambers and greys in regal colours. A torrent of bony spikes sprang suddenly and whistled through the air with a shrill yell like a battle cry, bombarding the hostel's shield in great numbers.

"That explains the skeletal porcupines," said Butler calmly commentating the scene to his giant rabbit friend.

Tovey chuckled, "You really are secretly brave aren't you," he said. "I'm positively petrified and you're commenting on the handy use of skeletal porcupines."

"I wonder if they'd work for me some time," pondered Butler unfazed, fine tuning the telescope.

There was one last surprise ready to enter the battlefield in the sky.

The golden amber grey became overshadowed by a darkness welling up in the clouds. A great waterfall of golden rain went up. From within it, something shaped like a mountain could be seen growing and stretching out. The golden wall of water began firing purple and black flames, hitting both the enemy and its own boney comrades. The great skeleton dragon roared and flew up as the golden wall exploded like an expensive firework. It was not life-sized or at least not fully grown, but nonetheless, awfully terrifying for the two tiny creatures hiding behind a flimsy magic wall that had already started to crack. The skeleton dragon soared across the makeshift battlefield like an ill-mannered bird, spitting fire everywhere, and making rather a nuisance of itself to the army it had been summoned to lead.

The skeleton army meanwhile tried their best to ignore it, dutifully continuing their pursuit of the Orakci. Understandably, the giant had grown rather tired with it all and had started stamping down one skeleton after another, stooping low and swinging its great big arms like clubs. The skeletal wolves charged blindly at the Orakci's feet, snapping at its toes as swarms of skeletal bats and eagles created a mess of an attack at the giant's head, arguing with one another as much as they laid their claws on the gentle giant.

"Dawei must be sad that Chise's gone," said the kedi sympathetically.

Tovey grumbled, "So he wants to rip her back out again. We don't even know what will happen if an Orakci dies. It's a horribly ill omen."

"As ill an omen as a magically summoned skeleton army?" replied Butler handing Tovey the telescope.

Tovey grunted lifting the telescope to his eye and taking over the commentary.

Just as the skeleton army was really starting to enjoy their work, many began retreating back as if scared of the well-natured giant. The skeletal warriors turned even more white, gaping in terror and looking at the hostel.

"The skeletons aren't looking at my floating house in the sky, are they?" asked the kedi to the rabbit.

"There's something behind us," replied the Magic Rabbit with dread.

A last skeleton, slow on the uptake, looked over the clouds from the giant's head and in terror shouted, "Hoomans! Hoomans! It's the end of the worlds!"

Soon the cries of the lone skeleton and the army could be heard no more, for both were drowned in the exploding barg of a missile that plummeted the Orakci's head down through the blanket of clouds. A twinkling of lights danced off and dispersed from within the giant's body that fell silently and slowly sank through the clouds, never to return to the Twilight again. In an instant, the sky filled with the deafening roar of armoured planes as they tanked through the confused ranks of Dawei's living dead army. Skeleton heads rolled and bones fell in showers, turning back to dust. This was no less alarming for the kedi and the rabbit of course. After all, in a few minutes, the hoomans could very well choose to turn to the magical house floating nonchalantly in the sky.

Tovey shrieked and then coughed as if to hide it, "This is our chance. Let's escape now. I can rebuild the hostel but I can't rebuild you!" he shouted panicked, pulling Butler away from the window.

When should I tell him?

The kedi followed and the two companions started running down to the last resort magical trap door that lead out to the abandoned library at the edge of the Twilight. As they reached it, the hostel's walls shrank and wobbled, helping the magical barrier take a particularly unwanted explosion. Tovey started climbing down the ladder in haste but Butler did not join him. He stood there, looking down at the rabbit and with a wave of paw, great big chains flickered into view.

Tovey looked up wide eyed as utter panic and horror fell upon his heart, "Wha..."

"The worlds outside the hostel are reserved for the living," announced Butler coldly, kicking Tovey with uncanny strength.

The kedi closed the trapdoor as the rabbit fell in shock, surrounded by distracting colours and the distinctive echoing click of the lock.

"Butler!"

Thirteen

Yesterday's Enemy, Today's Friend

Now dear reader, you may be curious about these so called hoomans and how they seem to be popping up just about everywhere these days. You see, there had been many murmurings from untrusted high officials of a possible invasion from Topside. It had indeed been in the news for the last half year or so and the wise creatures of the World Beneath had simply laughed at such a folly. An invasion? From hoomans? Even if they could, why in the earth would they want to do such a thing? And yet, the hoomans came. The hoomans came to Butler's very doorstep through the magic hour that had momentarily opened the gate to our beloved Twilight World. This is how the Hostel to Another World found itself in the very middle of an aerial battle between skeletons and hoomans. Or perhaps dear reader, it would be more befitting to call this charade a hunt, a hunt for the Angel of Death.

The hoomans were largely tucked away, deep inside experimentally equipped planes so they did not feel the strong foreboding breezes from the four winds. They had been flying through the magic hour for well over an hour now and those soldiers who had remained sceptical were now feeling rather exhilarated by the idea that they might in fact get to witness a new world. A few were walking along their large tin can of a plane, watching the clouds bathed in golds and oranges, pretending to inspect equipment. It was a pleasant pastime and many felt far more at ease now that they were away from the earth. They were the reserve force and not only that, instead of fighting in real wars, they were up in the clouds chasing magical creatures that didn't exist. How splendid! Two soldiers walked along happily passing the windows, looking out at the blanket of crimson clouds sleeping beneath them. Sometimes they felt as if they could see a blackening in the distance but now it was hidden once more, concealed by the brightness of the sun.

"I definitely saw it that time," said one. "There's definitely something in these clouds! I'm not mad. Maybe it's not a magical hostel but there is something up here."

"Maybe we can have a holiday there on our next annual leave," said the other.

"Maybe there's a cute monster girl who can serve us some beer from another world," replied the first. "I heard we're hunting a king. Or a future king at least."

"A king?" said the other sarcastically. "Just a murderer playing magic tricks who's been killing as he liked up until now. Kings are for fairytales."

An ear piercing alarm promptly started yelling at them, flashing angry red lights from above. To the two hoomans' surprise, a great explosion had appeared on a plane to their right side and a shadowed spec could be seen flying upwards through the amber glow.

"The King! The Angel of Death!" they shouted. "There's a new world in the sky!" they cried in excitement as all soldiers ran to the windows.

One can forgive such an unrestrained excitement and enthusiasm for a battle. After all, seeing a flying monster soar through the skies was not simply the beginning of another battle, it was the beginning of a life where magic exists.

The pure joy was short lived of course as a fellow pointed and shouted, "Either I'm going senile or that's a skeleton dragon coming for us!" he cried. "Prepare the stolen weapons! To your posts! Let's go! Let's go!"

Warning sirens were sounding, and bleeping, and echoing all along the hooman planes to remind the soldiers that they were in fact very much in danger. The smiling stopped and the laughter was replaced with a fear of the unknown.

The skeleton dragon meanwhile had been pleasantly cruising along following its master and was a little late to the hooman ambush. By the time it had arrived, it found for itself some very well prepared and brave hoomans ready to hunt them both down. Dawei flew with the wind and before long, all that could be seen of him was an elusive spec between the clouds.

"Focus on the dragon!" shouted a commanding officer already losing sight of their great catch of an angel. "I don't feel like being burnt alive in this tin can today my boys! Fire!"

The hoomans were very prepared. Every stolen weapon was warmed up and every hooman was ready for the victory looting of magical objects as gifts for their loved ones back on the earth. As the roar of the skeleton dragon's leisurely approach grew louder, the clouds began to flow and ripple from the careless shots of black fire and the beating of its wings. Through the wailing of sirens and the quiet focus of the hoomans, the dragon swept over them, towards the biggest of the weapons.

Dawei didn't like this at all. His thoughts were hazy and illformed but the facts remained clear: the hoomans were numerous and these strange enemies were stupid enough to fight a skeleton army in the sky. What if hoomans really did have weapons that could kill an angel? If he flew recklessly, he would likely be shot down with something rather nasty indeed. Huffing his frustrations, the angel doubled back towards the hostel. That was an easier target.

Dawei looked out over his makeshift battlefield and despaired. His skeletons were jumping back into the clouds and were being hunted down to dust on every side. Weapons had been abandoned. Even the skeletal wolves were in disarray, unable to lay a single bite on the planes circling around them. Some porcupines took down a plane before being wiped out in a single explosion. Even the skeleton dragon was flying erratically, hoping to get away amongst the confusion to save itself. This was the hooman's hope of course.

Die had just as much patience for an army of skeletons as she did for the obnoxious bleeping sirens that her superior had insisted on. The skeletons could all flee for all she cared. There was only one creature she was here to see. Almost all of the hoomans had started chasing the skeleton dragon, picking off the little skeletons as they went along. Die was not surprised. Common hoomans could be forgiven for getting distracted by a living dead dragon. Besides, they could keep it distracted and in turn would stay out of her way.

The hostel still stood with its crumbling magical barrier and a few tricks up its sleeve. A selection of ferret archers held their ground among the burning bricks that were being flung past their noses out through the barrier towards unsuspecting skeletons. They watched as the Angel of Death started eating the magical barrier with shamefully poor table manners. The ferret's captain was the legendary Dotty, and she of course knew that her friends were very ready to disappear back down the see-through coloured pipes regardless of the raise that they had been promised. The ferrets did not believe in it for one moment, although they did know Dotty herself was true to her word. Dotty held on tightly to a tiny beautiful bow and a needle like sword that had been fashioned from the holy fires of the Children of Light that very morning.

"Dawei's closing in. Archers at the ready," she announced trying to sound authoritative.

She watched from the corner of her eye as her companions began quietly slipping away to the safe comforts of the post office at the edge of the Twilight. Sighing, she readied her bow for what felt like the last time. *Goodbye Cian. Thank you.*

In that moment, out of the very dust dancing in the air, a tiny golden light in the shape of a ferret fluttered to her ear. She was not surprised and even pouted a little. *Where are you Mr Great Magician? You always disappear and reappear at the most inconvenient moments.*

The light hovered by her little ferret ear and spoke, "I'm running late. Apologies my dear Dotty. I suppose the others have already given up on that promotion," it said to her. "Not to worry. At least the little kedi is doing a marvellous job catapulting bricks and furniture. It's confusing the hoomans mighty well! Now listen closely, yesterday's enemy is today's friend. Look to hit our friend Dawei right through his hooman paw. It should slow him and whack a little bit of sense back in him. With any luck, Butler will make the right choice too. No time to explain! Will see you shortly, much love!"

Dotty attempted to squash the ferret light in her little ferret paws, missing spectacularly. She cursed as the golden ferret did a little sarcastic bow and disappeared. *What a peculiar man.* She smiled and drew the bow-string to her ear, ready to shoot an angel.

Dawei gnawed and ripped off pieces of the barrier. With one particularly messy bite, he tore through and dived with his hooman paw reaching out as if to pluck Dotty right off her perch. The little ferret fired and the arrow twanged. It whistled straight and unwavering as if dutifully following a path to the very centre of Dawei's palm. Dawei's skeletal wings faltered as he screamed in surprise, a scream that tore at the poor little ferret's heart.

"I'll leave the rest to you Boss," she said to the wind, hugging her bow tight and disappearing down the nearest pipe. "Be safe Butler. May Kurbaga be with you."

The scream hit Butler's ears and he ran over to the window to see Dawei writhing in the air, turning over and over, coiling and uncoiling. Their eyes met: the eyes of a scared little kedi and the eyes of a scared skeletal boy. Dawei looked at the creature who had been the last to see her. With droplets falling upwards he hissed his pain and flew towards the window at great speed, skeletal hand outstretched. Butler watched the angel plummet towards him, silhouetted in the golden amber rays of the Twilight. In a moment's time, those skeletal wings would crash through the glass and he would be face to face with the Angel of Death.

"Step back you idiot, he's come to kill you," came a voice from his pocket.

The little golden dragon flew out and transformed into the pink haired girl with the golden eyes of a serpent. Her blazing eyes caught Butler's attention and he let her pull him away. Still dazed he tripped clumsily, falling painfully onto his bottom and hitting the back of his head on the bar.

Dawei looked out towards the Twilight as a great boom shattered the remaining barrier. Falling through the air, he spread his wings wide, crashing down through the window and walls in spectacular fashion. He completely covered Butler as he fell and the raining bricks bounced off his skeletal wings. As Dawei crouched over the kedi and the girl, he looked innocently from the Angel Killer to the lollipops lying on the hostel floor. The battle roared outside as the kedi looked up at the 'killer' who had just saved his life. With fear welling up inside his soul, Butler searched behind him and felt the Angel Killer under his paw. With a deep breath, he firmed his grip and pointed a little object at the Angel of Death. The angel reached out with his hooman paw that still fashioned a needle like arrow and took the lollipop.

"No blood," Butler frowned, reaching out to retrieve Dotty's arrow.

"Would you stop trying to touch dangerous things," Silence protested, pulling Butler back, wondering how in the worlds he had survived all this time without her.

As Dawei thought to go hunt some hoomans, a silver thread appeared. It flickered happily from his wrist, dancing past Butler's outstretched fingers and stretching towards the Twilight.

The boy stared intently at it with a fierce gaze, letting his skeletal fingers caress the thread, "Chi-se," came a broken voice from behind the mask.

Butler and Silence watched wide eyed as the last of the madness disappeared from the boy's face. This was no king. This was just a lost skeletal boy, looking at his guiding light.

The boy jumped up, spreading his skeletal wings as far as they would go. A vast explosion shattered them as his expression turned white and the world turned black with gunpowder. There was a dull hissing, a whirl of wind, and a deadly silence. Butler shouted mutely as the boy fell out of sight through the wave of crimson clouds that welcomed him.

Fourteen

A Sea of Fire

The Children of Light became frenzied in anger and burst out of the hostel's veins, filling all the sky with a great burning. The clouds were overtaken by fire and shone deep crimson as though drenched in blood. The embers glowed across like a sea of fire and the hooman planes took on their new colour, reflecting the spirits' light. This was how the humble Battle of the Twilight came to an end with not one skeleton left to tell the tale. The hastily summoned army had embarrassingly started falling apart in the hoomans' hunt, and then quite unluckily, had found themselves drowning in angry swirling flames. Even the great skeleton dragon, fighting dreadfully outnumbered, fell into fiery waters, returning to the dust it once came.

The radios across the World Beneath were announcing I told you sos, giving live coverage of the Battle of the Twilight - the spark to ignite a war of the worlds. This was rather alarming indeed. Topsiders had never successfully entered the Twilight before, having always failed miserably, and there were alarming whispers of a traitor! The World Beneath was now looking for someone to blame, for the evil accomplice who had abandoned the World Beneath to scheme with hoomans.

Butler walked towards the door of the hostel and was now numb beyond joy or sorrow. The floating house in the sky had become more like a castle in ruins with holes of all shapes and sizes littering its walls and floorboards. In fact, the locker of treasures had simply disappeared entirely, and there was very little of the hostel left at all.

How dare one day be so busy.

The little kedi grumbled as he opened the hostel door. He had a job to do. The clouds of fire were now trying to eat the hooman planes and so one would think that a little kedi coming out of a floating house in the sky would have been easily overlooked. Butler looked over, and the last shreds of hope died in his heart. His fate was sealed. His chains bore heavy as he stepped out to complete Kurbaga's task.

"Let me walk out," he said to the Children of Light calmly.

The little embers filled with a new found fury yelled their protests. "Let me walk out and keep my heart beating," said the kedi, putting a paw to his shirt pocket. "This won't take long. I'll reward you with the finest logs the Twilight can provide. You know I would never ask you to help me risk disappearing for eternity unless it was for something important."

Butler spoke with authority and with clear mind as he looked out at the hooman figure waiting for him, standing on top of the plane's wing like a hero from a storybook. Before long, he would betray himself and the World Beneath would turn against him. The peaceful life that he'd dreamed of as a small kedi had long since slipped from his grasp, but he was being given a second chance at life. Indeed, his hostel was still standing and he was still technically in existence. There was hope yet of being unchained from the Hostel to Another World. In all the worlds, there had to be someone who could stitch him back together with a full soul and heart. *Why should I live as a shell of a body, eternally serving Master's hostel?* He stepped out of the door and walked slowly across the fiery waters.

Butler's thoughts turned to Tovey, but he felt no comfort from it, only dread of losing yet another friend. As he drew closer to the great hooman plane, he saw the Children of Light closest blackening and moving erratically. He felt himself as becoming blackened also, as if he were distorting into a sad shadow of the kedi he had wanted to become. In that moment of torment, it was memories of simpler times that helped him put one step in front of the other. Deep down he knew.

As if listening to his thoughts the little dragon spoke quietly from within her pocket, "We're not strong enough to be heroes. Just do what she says."

The kedi patted his pocket gently saying nothing and looked towards the hero standing perfectly balanced on a dreadfully untrustworthy hooman plane.

"Hello Die and welcome to the Twilight World. Don't shoot, if that's not too much to ask," he said as a greeting, putting his paws up in the air.

That was right, deep down he knew that he was not large enough to deal with such an unfair situation. If siding with hoomans was the only way to become a real living kedi again, he would gladly betray the World Beneath that had already abandoned him.

Although all the old passageways and magical installations were covered in debris or destroyed, and although all the hostel had holes blasted on the pesky whim of hoomans, Tovey knew every passage and every shortcut like the back of his paw.

"Stupid cat," grumbled the Magic Rabbit. "Stupid stupid stupid."

He climbed over all manners of objects that he hoped were not alive, and turned, and climbed yet again, and finally found himself a set of stairs. These were relatively clean and seemingly unused, and looked to be a DIY project almost complete yet forgotten at the last moment. "What a waste. I'll drag you out of this hostel by your ankles if I have to you daft cat! Not alive, hah! My bruised ribs have something to say to that Mr I'm Going To Sound So Cool kitty cat!"

Up, up, up Tovey went, gladly meeting no sign of a forgotten living thing, only dust bunnies that fled from his large clumsy hops. The steps were not made for a Magic Rabbit. "Just when did you start making things that could never be used by someone like me?" mused the rabbit sadly as he reminisced of an older better time.

He hopped and climbed all the same, and just as Tovey was feeling sombre and out of breath, the opening of the roof sprang into view from behind the wedged basket of an obnoxiously colourful weather balloon. The darkened crimson rays could be seen sneaking through the small space above Tovey's head and the air smelt of ashes.

Tovey hopped the last steps towards the light and squeezed through the small opening the basket cared to allow. "Holy guacamole," he said calmly at the calamity in front of him.

The roof had started early. "A secret staircase to the bar ay?" chuckled the rabbit rubbing the back of his neck as the breeze tried to unbalance him - a foolish endeavour.

Tables were burning and laden with what looked like arrows, but were in fact the poorly aimed porcupine quills made of bone. The chairs that had survived were lying broken and overturned in a mess of singed floorboards while plates and broken glasses lay in strangely tidy heaps. In fact, the only thing that seemed to have escaped the hoomans was the wildcat at the window that still stood proudly guarding at the one intact side of the hostel. As Tovey stood there feeling rather exhausted by the thoughts of repairs, a sound of crazed whispers fell upon his ears and the orange glow grew, calling for his immediate attention.

"What's wrong with you?" asked Tovey sceptically to the nearest Children of Light as he looked out across the sea they had created. "And where's that daft cat? I need to have a word with him."

The Children hissed menacingly and murmured, pulsing across the sky. It seemed almost as if someone had put them under an ancient spell and carved it through their very bodies by forbidden words of old. Tovey waved a paw of impatience at them and picked up the telescope, careful to poke it first. It wouldn't bode well to burn his paw at such an important time. As he looked out over the crimson clouds, he could roughly see two figures, one standing on the fire and the other standing on a plane. "What is he doing?" he mumbled. "We're not in a super-hero book. What idiot walks out on a sea of fire in the sky to talk to hoomans?"

The greyness left in the clouds was fading as the sun sent its warm light with rays of gold that fell like raindrops. A flurry of frightened fish flew through the smoke and gave Tovey a little scare before continuing their search for a release from the embers. Tovey stood gazing out with dazzled eyes, trying to understand what on earth could be happening. "I've only been gone an hour!" he huffed indignantly. "Don't even try to push me off wind. You won't manage," he muttered as the four winds continued biting at his fur.

The Magic Rabbit could now clearly see the little dark silhouette of the kedi and that of another who now walked across blackened flames towards him. Soon they both stood on black swirling embers that coiled around Butler's legs in their distress, pulling him desperately back towards the floating house in the sky. The foreign figure stopped in front of the kedi and was now leaning closer still. Tovey watched as Butler paused and fiddled in his jacket for a moment. "What are you doing? What is he doing?" he asked the Children of Light again to no reply. He gasped, "That's the Angel Killer, and the Map of the Worlds!"

Indeed, there was no mistaking them, even at such a distance. Butler was giving the hooman two of the most dangerous items in all the worlds. "Butler, you fool!" he boomed stomping involuntarily. "It's that weird woman isn't it?" he asked to the air, studying the second figure.

The hooman leant into Butler and pointed the Angel Killer at his head as a secret conversation took place. "Oh Kurbaga no no no!" shouted the rabbit as he dropped the telescope and delved hurriedly, searching for something in his magical pouch. "Can you at least bring over what they're saying on the air?" he asked the Children of Light who hissed back up at him. "Oh you're useless," he snapped at them as his bunny cheeks reddened and his heartbeat sped ever quicker. "Got it!"

Tovey took aim with a large Magic Rabbit sized crossbow, hoping desperately that he still remembered how to use it. Thank goodness it was a newer model and had a long range lens included for the bargain sale price. With trembling giant fluffy paws, Tovey rested and steadied the crossbow on a broken piece of wall, loading it with the only arrow he could find. He could have sworn he'd bought a few of them.

"Oh bother!" he barked at himself in frustration as he almost dropped both arrow and crossbow.

With a deep breath and renewed focus, Tovey the Magic Rabbit aimed a weapon for the first time at a real life living thing, terrified of the praying he would be doing to ask for forgiveness later. "I'm sorry Kurbaga. I can't let my friend die. Please lend me your strength."

There was a loud swish as the arrow flashed in the colours of the rainbow from the sudden impact of the magical trigger. It was rather pretty in fact, although that was not the reason Tovey had chosen this model of course.

"Did it work?" he asked the winds with trembling paws.

Tovey stiffly held the crossbow at his good eye and watched in cold dread as the hooman, with mildly bleeding cheek, lifted her free arm. The plane steadied onto its new target and Tovey, smiling slightly at his own incompetence, looked to his friend who was now shouting incomprehensibly at him across the sky.

"I'm sorry old friend. I guess I really couldn't save you in the end," laughed Tovey sadly, unblinking, not willing to lose even a second. "Goodbye old friend. I..."

The air filled with an explosion of horrors and a silence worse than death settled upon the burning skies of the Twilight.

Fifteen

The Beginning of the End

There was a great light. The white orb sped and expanded until it was too big to contain itself, exploding inwardly with the power to vaporise an army. All fell to their versions of ground, so fierce was its light. Hanging ominously in the sky, the orb continued spouting white sparks into the air, spinning over and over as the sky heaved from its pull. Seeking to settle the light's anger, a vast fog leaped from the clouds, filling the space in a mysterious white, as all unfortunate to be present prayed for a miraculous end.

"Am I dead?" asked the Magic Rabbit.

"Yes," came a voice with a hint of a smile.

Tovey uncurled to place himself more comfortably and had a little look about. There was a thick fog now and yet the figure floating next to him stretching out its long limbs could only be him.

"Hello pesky Magician. I'm not dead am I?"

Cian did a little skip in the air, "I'll leave that for you to decide Mr Magic Rabbit," he laughed before a much more sinister look came over him. "Let's bid farewell to our unwelcome guests shall we?"

With a click of his fingers, the Magician pushed the mists back through the clouds to reveal his mischief. Tovey looked down and caught his breath as he took in the view. The great light shone a mere two metres from a hooman plane, snapping at its wing. Its core fizzed a vibrant rainbow, as it took in all that fell upon it, transforming the unfortunate into tens of thousands of angry white sparks. There came a rushing of magic, a silent rolling of living fire as the orb called the Children of Light to take their free samples of magical power. Tovey watched the sea of fire below him rise and rush towards the orb in great heaving waves as rainbow flames flooded the Twilight with renewed vigour. Tovey peered wide eyed as glimmers of giant white ferrets charged towards the hoomans, calling the renewed embers with a squeaky battle cry. The two planes that were still hovering in the clouds were understandably petrified and disappeared very quickly indeed. No one wants to be chased by ferret beasts burning brighter than the sun whilst drowning in a flood of rainbow fires after all. Those hoomans that had fallen behind drew back in hast, having received the message loud and clear - they had outstayed their welcome. Cian stood stoically, sternly looking over to Die. She removed the Angel Killer from Butler's temple still smiling, even daring to take her time, whispering unknown words into the kedi's ear. The kedi nodded obediently and bowed low until the plane retreated out of sight.

So it was, that the last hooman plane veered downwards through the clouds of the Twilight as the rushing flood of rainbow fire and white light engulfed the sky. With a last wave of rushing flames, the engine's rumble soon became drowned in the serene happiness of the light. Tovey felt himself falling and the happiness of children's laughter seemed to well up inside him, swallowing him together with the enemy. He fell into the peacefulness of darkness and saw no more. With a flick of the wrist, the light swiftly returned to Cian's palm and he grinned thoroughly satisfied.

"Come on back now you little rascals," Cian called out to the Children of Light. With a last swirling dance, the embers happily returned home with kedi in tow, ready for a well deserved rest.

Creatures of the Twilight soon ventured out across the clouds and greeted the Magician and the kedi, who happily led them up into the remains of the hostel for a spot of tea or perhaps something stronger. There, a warm welcome was made under the golden sun, and many eager tufted ears bought the last surviving bottles, seeking to hear more of the war hungry creatures named the hoomans. It was Cian who told his story of this hooman encounter, for Butler was feeling rather drowsy all of a sudden after all that excitement. Many of the events in the adventure he knew, for he had been an unfortunate main character in them. But, there came moments where he listened very carefully indeed, for there were many things he had missed entirely. It was in that gathering with tea in paw that he discovered where Cian had disappeared to. The Magician proudly recounted the story to the gathered creatures, of how he had been floating in the clouds when coins and objects started to rain all around him. Cian had thought this rather odd behaviour and had started collecting them, recognising certain objects from when he had looked after Butler as a cub.

"Aren't there more monies here than before?" asked Butler groggily as he ventured out back where the Magician had dumped it all.

Cian laughed, "You're imagining things. The hostel has space yet to grow into the home of many I daresay," said the Magician warmly. "As the East seeks to be freed after many long years, I do hope the rest of the worlds will choose to come together and drink tea with our very own dear Butler of the Hostel to Another World! Yet I do believe skeletons need to be banished from the worlds. They stole my armoured hot air balloon."

"You mean the one that you stole from the hoomans when they weren't paying attention?" Butler chuckled. "It would be nice if someone would call this place home," he sighed, "but I fear that is too hopeful a thought," said the kedi.

"No one stays," piped up his pocket helpfully to which it got a firm pinch.

When the stories of the adventures had been told, there came yet more stories and Butler's head fell sideways onto Tovey's warm fluffy chest. He snored quietly, kicking occasionally in his sleep. The kedi's dreams played him scenes of Tovey leaving and enveloped him in darkness, a darkness he knew very well. But there were also dreams of happier times and memories long forgotten. Butler smiled in his sleep as a very small Tovey refused to jump off a set of three baby steps and he did it, him. He was a brave little kedi.

Butler awoke to find himself on a half burnt bed with the golden hour shining through a wall full of holes. From out of the open window could be heard many a creature singing heartfelt prayers of peace from the edges of the clouds as they waited for the train. There was a huff and a squeak of a chair that protested under the large bottom that sat upon it. Butler's round hazel eyes stared.

"Up you get, you don't plan to sleep all day do you?" asked the Magic Rabbit gruffly. "Up we go. Take my paw."

"Don't leave me, please. Tovey I'm sorry," said the kedi quietly.

"I'm scared, I'm scared, I'm scared," piped up his pocket.

There was a wriggle and the tiny golden dragon poked its nose out, giving an excellent rendition of those same round pleading eyes, sneezing a couple of sparks for good measure.

"I'm here. Don't look at me like that, that's unfair! I need to go for a little while but I will never leave you. I don't forgive you for what you did mind you, not yet. But, there are many things I don't understand and you're more important to me than those things. Come now."

With a heave, Tovey was able to pull the kedi up. Butler avoided the rabbit's gaze and placed the wriggling Silence next to the glass of milk and plate of biscuits that lay on the strangely intact bedside table. "You really do like getting yourself into all the troubles don't you Mr Cat? Of all the daft creatures you are the daftest of all Butler!' said Tovey. "And you owe me your finest breakfast after flinging me out of your secret trapdoor. My ribs man! You daft cat!" complained the rabbit indignantly. "You always try and do everything yourself. That's stupid, trying to go against an army without me and all. What would you have done if I hadn't come back?"

"Cian would have saved me like he always does," giggled Butler cheekily, coming back to himself.

"Saved!" boomed Tovey. "That ridiculous magician would have blown up the whole Twilight if I hadn't been next to him! What if something had happened to you? What would I do then? It would have…" he trailed off looking at his lap.

"Following me almost killed you Tovey," said Butler quietly. "I will never let that happen."

"Not as bad as being kicked out," huffed Tovey childishly.

"It is far worse! The World Beneath is going to hate me Tovey. The Holy Priesthood will hate me."

"I know. I know, okay?" replied the Magic Rabbit heavily.

Tovey plopped his bottom down to the protest of the chair and paused to ruffle the dragon's chin. "I know you're now the traitor. Of course you are after what you did. But I'm not leaving you, come what may of it."

"Now don't go saying that now and get scared later Mr Fancy Priestly Rabbit," coaxed the kedi quietly.

"I won't let anyone hate you," answered Tovey. "I won't let you walk this alone. I'll knock some sense into all the priests of the Holy Church if I have to."

Butler laughed heartily at this. A warmth filled the kedi and his heart who now gladly pushed her face into the glass of milk, wagging her dragon's tail softly as she drank.

"Leave for now and do what you need to do," smiled Butler. "We'll need help. Don't make any enemies you don't have to. I know how bad your temper is Mr Holy Rabbit."

Tovey slapped Butler's arm playfully, almost pushing him off the bed, "Just you hold on tight and fix up that bar. I'll come back before you know it with some good news and we can have a drink like old times!" beamed Tovey as he stood to leave.

"I'll be here like always," replied the kedi. "Thank you Tovey. I, I am scared," he said shyly, "but I'm so happy to have you," he said burying his head in his paws with tufted ears turning a fetching red. "I'm glad. Let's find a way! We will find a way to escape this war and may all the creatures find their safe place. Cian will look after the World

Beneath I'm sure. I don't suppose he will pop up as often. He might get very busy."

"I think he'll pop up Mr Butler. I think he'll pop up so much in fact that you'll be chasing him out with a broom," said the rabbit quite seriously. "You don't really believe that Cian would miss even a single one of your adventures, do you? Now, you are surprisingly strong for a creature so small and you are a good kedi Butler. You know I like you a lot," started Tovey.

"I like you more," replied the kedi automatically, grinning happily to himself.

"I like you most!" retorted the Magic Rabbit. "Ahem, so as I was saying, I like you very much, but do remember, you are only a small kedi. You don't need to be a hero Butler."

"And thank the Master and the Skeleton King for that!" laughed the kedi.

Butler was alone once more and all was quiet but for the soft snoring of a very contented little dragon. As he stood there and braced himself for the biggest clean since Cian mistakenly sneezed too hard, he decided to have a look out of the window to see the extent of the inconvenient damage. The kedi watched the Twilight World in all its golden crimson splendour, with shoals of flying fish returning to the clouds. A great sky whale could be seen in the distance, diving down into the sea of clouds, happy to have been left in peace once more. There was a strange spec that Butler couldn't quite make out. Something was floating uncharacteristically as if it were waiting. The kedi thought it safest to leave it be, but it was in that moment that a giant mass of dark clouds formed in the shape of a skeleton hand. Looking horribly out of place, it shot out over the blanket of crimson and grabbed the suspicious spec.

"What now?" huffed the kedi.

Two red laser eyes shone menacingly from the unnatural formation of cloud floating above the rest. They peered happily as if staring right at him, lifting the thing closer to the hostel, gazing at Butler for approval. The skeleton hand glided swiftly closer, ro more than a few metres away now, and Butler heard a weak cough with a soft clinking of bones. He stood with gaping jaw, drawing in a sharp breath. He stared at what the hand had gathered before looking back up to face the dark cloud that was patiently waiting. With tears in his eyes and a great big smile, Butler bowed his head as far as it would go. The red lights twinkled satisfied and diligently turned themselves off, swiftly taken over by the blanket of crimson once more. There was another weak cough and with a gentle motion, the skeletor hand turned away and disappeared deep into the clouds of the Twilight.

"See you again friend," said Butler as he turned away with a feint clinking of metal, ready to prepare the Hosel to Another World for its bumpy new chapter and the beginning of the war of the worlds. "Bother, how inconvenient!"

www.ingramcontent.com/pod-product-compliance
Lightning Source LLC
Chambersburg PA
CBHW031007210726
48290CB00007B/2518

* 9 7 8 1 7 3 9 1 3 1 1 0 4 *